Josee, the Tiger and the Fish

Seiko Tanabe

YEN
ON

New York

Josee, the Tiger and the Fish

Seiko Tanabe

Translation by Matt Rutsohn

JOZE TO TORA TO SAKANA TACHI
©Seiko Tanabe 1985, 1987
First published in Japan in 1985 by KADOKAWA CORPORATION, Tokyo. English translation rights arranged with KADOKAWA CORPORATION, TOKYO, through TUTTLE-MORI AGENCY, INC., Tokyo.

English translation © 2022 by Yen Press, LLC

Yen On
150 West 30th Street, 19th Floor
New York, NY 10001

Visit us at yenpress.com • facebook.com/yenpress • twitter.com/yenpress • yenpress.tumblr.com • instagram.com/yenpress

First Yen On Edition: March 2022

Yen On is an imprint of Yen Press, LLC.
The Yen On name and logo are trademarks of Yen Press, LLC.

Library of Congress Cataloging-in-Publication Data
Names: Tanabe, Seiko, 1928–2019, author. | Rutsohn, Matt, translator.
Title: Josee, the tiger and the fish / Seiko Tanabe ; translated by Matt Rutsohn.
Other titles: Joze to tora to sakana tachi. English
Description: First Yen On edition. | New York : Yen On, 2022.
Identifiers: LCCN 2021059105 | ISBN 9781975340452 (hardcover)
Subjects: LCGFT: Romance fiction. | Light novels. | Short stories.
Classification: LCC PL862.A48 J6913 2022 | DDC 895.63/5—dc23/eng/20220107
LC record available at https://lccn.loc.gov/2021059105

ISBNs: 978-1-9753-4045-2 (hardcover)
       978-1-9753-4046-9 (ebook)

10 9 8 7 6 5 4 3 2 1

LSC-C

Printed in the United States of America

Contents

I Can't Drink This Hot Tea

Yoshioka was wearing glasses when she saw him again that day, seven years later. He had grown old and weary, but the glasses were the most surprising change. Before she offered even a simple hello…

"Have you always worn glasses?!"

…Aguri couldn't stop herself from shouting.

"Nah, started wearing 'em 'round last year, I guess…"

Yoshioka's appearance had clearly changed. But it was more than just a young man reaching the prime of his life.

Do all men age this fast?

Yoshioka was still only thirty-six years old.

"Heh-heh… Heh-heh-heh…" Yoshioka chuckled as he took off his shoes. "Hey, uh… Can I come in? Huge place ya got here… A rental? Or didja buy it?" he asked, already making his way inside.

"Oh, please… Do you really think I could afford buying a place like this? I'm renting… Come on in."

Aguri showed him into a room across from the outside hallway. She was basically treating it as a place to entertain guests, but this dreary room was also where she usually held work meetings. People from television stations and film companies would pile in here to discuss business, filling the air with cigarette smoke. The white wallpaper had taken a light-brown tint as a result.

Aguri cleaned the place once a year on New Year's Eve, but even the rag she used had become discolored and gunked up to the point that she didn't really care enough anymore to decorate the room or make it look nice. Cluttered with various baubles and knickknacks she had lying around the house, it practically screamed *nothing beats cheap*. The walls were bare of any paintings—only a calendar pinned up with a thumbtack. She took notes on the calendar for work, which was why it had check marks and *X*s scribbled all over it in permanent marker.

One time, when Aguri was writing for a morning soap opera, the show's lead actress stopped by and said, "This place is way too dreary. Here, take this," and gifted her a flower vase.

Aguri had just bought some flowers to put in the vase, which was now atop the sideboard. She would never do something like that if a work colleague was visiting, but Yoshioka was different. They used to date, after all.

The room could use some color, she figured.

Aguri had actually considered putting the flowers in the living room out back and taking Yoshioka there. The living room was very sunny, with a great view of the mountains. It had beautiful curtains and furniture, too. But Aguri suddenly changed her mind and showed Yoshioka into the gloomy drawing room.

Yoshioka was wearing a navy-blue polo with a white cotton jacket and wrinkly ecru pants. His features were lined with age, so his fashionable getup didn't quite hit the mark. He just looked tired and shabby. Yoshioka was a shadow of his once-gentlemanly self—maybe his life had taken a turn for the worse—and yet his overall charm and endearing smile hadn't faded one bit.

That's how he gets you, thought Aguri.

Some people were hard to approach, but not Yoshioka. He was the definition of approachable, and that was what had made him so popular with women.

"Right... So this is where you work?" he asked.

Yoshioka took a seat on the couch and started curiously looking around. His curiosity turned to confusion when he noticed there wasn't a single picture or painting to look at.

"This is the drawing room," said Aguri. "I do my work down the hall."

"Bet you're really busy, writing for a TV show with a really popular actress and all. You make good money?"

"Enough to get by."

"You're a real big shot now. I can barely look ya in the eye, Aguri... Maybe I've said too much."

Aguri snorted, then took a seat in the chair across from Yoshioka. There was a television in the corner of the room, and in front of the TV stand was an award from the TV station's president congratulating Aguri on her show's high ratings. However, it was facing backward, so her guests would have no clue what it was for.

Yoshioka sat up straight once again.

"Been so long that I dunno where to start... How many years now?" he asked.

"Six or seven, maybe?" Aguri replied, even though she knew it had been exactly seven years since they broke up. She picked up the kettle she always kept on the side table and started pouring tea. "So," she began, "what made you decide to call me out of the blue like that? I was surprised, to say the least."

"Heh-heh... Heh-heh-heh..."

Aguri noticed that Yoshioka's face seemed more scrunched up, and his forehead wrinkled like a monkey's when he laughed. Perhaps he'd lost weight. It was a slight turnoff, so she looked away. But she knew his body very well. She could still remember every curve from his neck to his shoulders and how it felt to run her hands down them, although her raw affection for Yoshioka had long faded. It was now a mere memory.

I can't believe it's been so long...

Listening to him talk felt like hearing a long-forgotten song being played on an old, broken jukebox. That one night last week, his voice had made Aguri's heart skip a beat—unlike now.

It had been around eight PM when the phone rang.

"Uh...I'm trying to reach Aguri Takao, the writer for Mother Tan-tan. *Is this the right number?"*

It was a man. Fans of the show *Mother Tantan* had managed to get a hold of Aguri's phone number in the past, so she replied in a deep, stiff voice, "Yes, it is."

Some people had even called to tell her how much they hated her show, a serial TV dramedy about a single-mother household.

"Yeah...that's Aguri, all right. Guess who this is."

"Who?"

"Ya really can't tell, huh? It's...it's me, Yoshioka."

Aguri had figured it out before he said his name. She felt her heart pound in her chest. Most likely a conditioned response—an old habit.

"Sorry for callin' outta nowhere. Ya busy right now?"

"Yes, I am. What do you want?"

She always acted like this while she was working, but it flustered Yoshioka.

"I'm really sorry for interrupting, then. Actually, there's somethin' I wanna talk about. Think we could get together?"

"When?"

"Whenever's good for you. It's, uh... It's kinda hard askin' this, since you're famous and all now, but...think ya could make a li'l time to meet up with this fella?"

"Meet up with this fella" made it sound like Yoshioka was talking about someone else, but he was in fact referring to himself. He talked just the same as always. Aguri wanted to laugh; it brought back so many memories.

"Sure. I can't this week, though. Way too busy."

"That's fine. Any time's good."

"I'm only free next Wednesday."

"Arright. What time Wednesday?"

Aguri figured Yoshioka wouldn't be able to meet during the day if he was working, but she didn't want to meet at night, either. She didn't know why one of her exes wanted to see her, and she worried what would happen if he came over at night with food and alcohol. Aguri had no intention of ever getting back together with Yoshioka. Plus, she was somewhat suspicious of him.

Yoshioka had inherited his family's business, although Aguri heard that it folded only two years after he took over. She thought that maybe he was going to ask her for something. At least, that was what her instincts as a thirty-two-year-old woman were telling her.

"How about two o'clock?" she suggested, to which Yoshioka immediately replied, *"Yeah, that's perfect. Can I meet you at your place?"*

"Um… What was it you wanted to talk about?"

"I'll tell ya in person. Anyway—man, it's been ages since I last heard your voice. You haven't changed a bit. How old are you again?"

"Does it matter how old I am?!"

"Oh, sorry. It's just—sheesh, your voice really brings back memories. Like, I honestly didn't think you'd wanna see me, so I figured I'd just give ya a call. Glad I got to talk to you. Thanks."

Even after hanging up, Aguri could still hear his "Glad I got to talk to you. Thanks" ringing in her head. She so seldom heard those words that they gave her an emotional rush. It had been a while since she'd felt such excitement.

Last year, she'd become close with one of the supporting actors on her show. He'd call her every time he was in Osaka and they'd go out for lunch, although things never went any further than that. Perhaps their relationship would have developed into something more, but Aguri was cautious and preferred work over dating and romance.

Around three or four years ago, she'd gone out with a man from a local television network, but he got transferred to their Nagoya office and she then grew extremely busy, so things naturally ended there. Now Aguri's entire life was work, but she found it fulfilling.

"Glad I got to talk to you. Thanks."

Yoshioka's voice resonated deep within her heart.

That's just the kind of guy he is, she said to herself. *He's so…*

He was self-centered. He'd said he was going to marry Aguri, when meanwhile, he'd had another woman on the side whom his parents were trying to get him to wed. And then, with a straight face, he'd told Aguri:

"Yeaaah, nah. I can't."

"Can't what?"

"Get married. To you."

"What?!" Aguri had blurted out. "Did you seriously just say, 'Yeaaah, nah' about something this important?"

But somehow, she couldn't hate the guy.

"Forgive me. I'm sorry."

Aguri felt weak in the knees when he said that.

"Really, I am."

She'd been working at city hall at the time, heartbroken to the point that she hadn't thought she'd have the strength to wake up every morning. But she'd needed this job to survive, so she poured all her energy into work. And even then, Aguri couldn't bring herself to resent Yoshioka. He wasn't capable of standing up to his parents; he panicked over the arranged marriage they were forcing him into and meanwhile found himself unable to break things off with Aguri. Nonetheless…

"What's this girl like?" Aguri asked.

"A real beauty," Yoshioka replied with utmost sincerity. Aguri was hit with the urge to murder him until he continued, "It hurts.

I wake up every morning hopin' it's all a dream, that it's you by my side instead, and I just can't stop crying."

He was actually crying, too.

"It kills me."

That was all it took for Aguri to forgive him.

"Well… Bummer…"

That out-of-date slang was the last thing she said to Yoshioka before cutting him out of her life. Even after getting an abortion, she still couldn't hate the man.

Her old boyfriend from the TV network clutched his stomach with laughter when she told him about Yoshioka.

"What an idiot. He couldn't stand up to his parents, then gets so haunted by his obligations and feelings that he starts crying? Sounds straight out of the works of Chikamatsu."

Then he started sarcastically saying, "It kills me," which ended up making Aguri more annoyed with him than anything else.

Who do you think you are? Oh, so he's the idiot? You think you're so great with your wife and kids, but here you are, leading a double life with me on the side.

Maybe it came down to chemistry. What Aguri had with Yoshioka in bed was perfect. They made love—sweet and gentle yet passionate love, as opposed to the aggressive, unflattering sex she had with the man from the television network. Perhaps those memories still lingered in the back of her mind, and her admiration, which was a mix between obsession and regret, was what was keeping her memories of Yoshioka from ever leaving her side.

Aguri never mentioned this to the man from the television network, but she was impressed that Yoshioka was the son of a CEO— granted, the CEO of a small enterprise with around two hundred employees. One day, when she and Yoshioka were passing by the company's factory in the Higashiyodogawa Ward in his car, he pointed at the tall fence and said:

"That's ours."

Aguri had various intentions of her own. She'd weighed the advantages and disadvantages of marrying Yoshioka, so maybe God had punished her for having such utilitarian motives. Deep down, she felt Yoshioka wasn't the only bad guy here.

Nevertheless, when she heard him say, "Glad I got to talk to you. Thanks" during their first phone call in ages, it reminded her of his "It kills me" all those years ago.

That's just the kind of guy he is, Aguri said fondly to herself. There was no doubt that when Yoshioka said something like that, he was speaking from the heart.

At any rate, what does he want to even talk about, especially after all these years?

Hearing Yoshioka's voice on the phone had raised Aguri's expectations far too high, because she was remembering the old him. But the real Yoshioka had aged, and his choice of glasses wasn't helping things. Aguri was disillusioned.

Yoshioka quietly watched her as she made tea, then shook his head.

"Ya haven't changed at all. Still as young and beautiful as ever."

"I wonder. They say women age faster if they work too much."

Aguri was wearing light makeup. Even though she never had the spare time to get a perm and simply got a monthly trim instead, her shoulder-length tresses were perfectly straight and glistening. She flipped her hair over her shoulder while making an effort not to meet Yoshioka's eye, since she could sense him staring at her.

When Aguri eventually looked at him, she could instinctively tell that he hadn't come over just to catch up on old times. But she still had no idea why he was here.

"Hard to believe six or seven years have passed…," Yoshioka said as he took a cigarette out of his pocket.

He's planning on overstaying his welcome, isn't he? thought Aguri, a touch despondent. After all, she had a few more scenes to write before the end of the day if she wanted to meet her deadline.

Yoshioka's fingers were thick like those of someone who worked in a field, and his fingernails were broken and rough. When he was younger, the backs of his hands had been soft and slightly plump, maybe because he'd been a bit chubby back then. They'd been pale like a woman's hands, his fingers similarly unblemished. His palms were so warm when he wrapped his hands around Aguri's that day years ago and said, "Whoa. Your hands are freezing. People say 'cold hands, warm heart,' and I reckon they might be right."

Aguri found his sweet-as-a-peach tone so sexy. Yoshioka was really good at gauging her mood whenever they made love. He was observant, sensitive, and gentle. Back where they were from in Osaka, people called anything syrupy sweet and gentle "sweet as a peach." That phrase fit Yoshioka to a T, from his personality to the way he talked and had sex.

But there was no trace of that quality now, which was why Aguri thought he looked different and seemed less gentlemanly.

"They keep tellin' me to lay off the cigarettes, but I can't... Same goes for booze. I'd be lost without it."

"Who's telling you that?"

"Doctors. Said I'm gonna fuzz up my liver."

People from Aguri and Yoshioka's hometown often said "fuzz up" to mean *mess up* or *damage in some way*. Aguri had spent most of her adult life in Tokyo by now, so it felt like ages since she'd last heard such slang.

"*Mother Tantan*'s a smash hit, eh? I love it."

"Thanks. But it's the actors who deserve all the credit."

"Nah, it's the script. I mean, I'm no expert or nothin', but still— you really hit the big leagues all of a sudden, y'know? That's proof you're talented."

"I just got lucky."

"You been writing since way back, too? I had no idea. When I first saw your name on the TV, I thought it was a completely different person, just with the same name. Then I saw your picture in a magazine two or three years ago. Boy, was that a surprise."

"…"

"But then I was like, 'Yeah, that makes sense…' You always were smart. Even the letters ya used to write me were really good."

"Did I used to write you letters?" Aguri asked, even though she clearly remembered doing so.

"Yeah, ya did, but when we broke up, I gave 'em back like you asked. You seriously don't remember? Unbelievable."

"Doesn't ring any bells. I probably threw them out."

That was a lie. Aguri hadn't looked at them in years, but they were still stowed away in a cardboard box in a storage unit. She kept the best of their correspondences bundled together.

"I never expected you'd get so famous. It's all about talent these days, y'know. Can't get rich without talent."

Yoshioka went to take a sip of the tea Aguri had made, but it must have been too hot, because he placed his cup back on the table.

The sound of children's footsteps and voices suddenly got louder before fading into the distance, since the apartment building's exterior passageway was right outside the window.

Yoshioka lowered his voice. "You, uh, got anyone here with ya? Or you live alone?"

"Just me."

"Still single?"

"Still single."

Yoshioka's eyes anxiously wandered behind his glasses. "…Seriously?"

"I'm married to my job… Ha-ha-ha."

Aguri giggled after remembering a conversation she'd had with the building's super on the first floor. Yoshioka was going to come over at two o'clock, so she went to go buy some flowers before he arrived. She figured she could at least decorate the place and show Yoshioka the living room, since she wasn't going to be entertaining him with food and drink. Her living room had a balcony facing the mountains, and Aguri had some of her favorite furniture there: a fluffy, white rug, a cabriole-legged couch with sky-blue satin uphol-stery, and a dark-green onyx table.

On the table was a white coffee cup, and tossed over the couch was a dark-navy negligee made of silk. One side of the room, where Aguri did her work, was cluttered with stacks of scripts and rough drafts, although she could hide all that by closing the accordion door.

Yoshioka's voice over the phone brought back so many fond memories that Aguri decided to catch up with him in the living room. She never brought anyone from work there.

When she returned to her apartment complex after buying flow-ers, she found the building's super waiting for her.

"Some strange man stopped by to see you," the woman explained. "He said he was a little early and you weren't home, so he asked if I could let him inside so he could wait there."

"What happened after that?"

"I told him I don't keep a master key anymore, so I can't let him in."

"Did he go home?"

"No, he said he was going to take a walk around the block and come back, but he kept asking these weird questions before he left. 'Is she married?' 'Does she live alone?' 'Does she have any kids?' 'Her last name is Takao, right?' It freaked me out. I thought he was a thief scoping places to rob, so I just kept telling him, 'I don't know.'"

Aguri immediately knew it was Yoshioka. He had a bad habit of asking innocent yet prying questions whenever he wanted to know something. He could be really persistent.

Aguri quickly changed her mind about bringing Yoshioka into her living room. All of this had reminded her that she hadn't seen him in seven years and that he was an enigma to her now. *Why go through all that trouble?* she figured.

She ended up putting just a few lilies and carnations in the gloomy drawing room, then she closed the divider between it and the living room.

Yoshioka must not have been satisfied with the super's answers, because he peppered Aguri with further questions.

"You're still single? Seriously?"

"I don't have time for a man. I've got work to do."

That response seemed to finally convince him.

"Makes sense... Been seein' your name everywhere these last two, three years, after all. You wrote a novel a little while ago, yeah? Haven't read it yet, though... What made ya start writing this much anyway? You got a good hand on ya."

"Got a good hand on ya" was Yoshioka's cute way of saying she was a talented writer.

Aguri had always wanted to write, ever since she was in high school. She'd gone to junior college—more like finishing school—but then attended screenwriting lectures after she started working. She even went to a comedy writing workshop and was eventually approached by the lecturer:

"You write the funniest dialogue. How about learning how to write for TV?"

For some reason, Aguri had good intuition, not so much talent. It probably had to do with how she was raised. Both of her parents had strong personalities—a little too strong, which was why they were always at each other's throats. Growing up with two angry adults in constant conflict made Aguri learn to keep her distance from others. Perhaps that was what led to her desire to write. The downfall of her relationship with Yoshioka had also pushed her to take a crack at screenwriting. Her run of good luck was tenuous at first, but eventually, her scripts turned a profit. One series in particular got popular enough for a publishing company to approach Aguri about a book deal. When she gave it a try, the result was even better than she'd imagined. After that, she found that she could take material too difficult to adapt for television and turn it into essays and novels. Some people told Aguri that she'd finally hit her stride, although she didn't feel that way herself. She secretly chalked it all up to her good intuition. Eager to strike while the iron was still hot, Aguri wanted to further hone her skills. She never once let her guard down, because she knew that doing so could be a death sentence in her line of work. It was feast or famine.

She felt like she was walking across a tightrope. Not that she would ever reveal as much to Yoshioka, however.

"I just got lucky. That's all," she insisted.

"I dunno about that."

"How'd you get my number anyway?"

"I called a newspaper company."

"Oh…"

"C'mon, you've gotta be making bank, living in a huge apartment like this. You got a vacation house, too?"

"Why do you ask?"

"Oh, it's just that when I saw you in that one magazine, you were in this beautiful room with a view of the mountains, drinking coffee or somethin'. Real luxurious. I was like, 'Man, she's living the high life.'"

"That's the room in the back. It's far from luxurious, though…"

Sure, there was a silk gown, a cabriole sofa, and a white coffee cup, and the view from the living room was just as beautiful as it looked in that women's fashion magazine. But Aguri never had the time to actually sit there in that gown and enjoy herself. The view was a pleasing visual no different from looking at pictures in a magazine.

Aguri worked day and night at her desk, and once she got tired, she'd collapse onto the perpetually unmade bed next to it. She fell asleep wearing the same clothes she worked in more often than not, which was why she wore a baggy cotton dress almost year-round. For food, she'd stop by the café on the first floor of her apartment complex, where she had a tab. She hardly even had the time to be disappointed about that anymore.

Aguri sat on her cabriole sofa drinking coffee in a nice, long dress only when magazine companies sent photographers to her place for pictures. Of course anyone who saw those photos would think she lived a luxurious life.

She didn't have a man she could complain to about her struggles. Nor would she ever talk to any of the male actors she occasionally met about something so personal. She'd once opened up to her TV network ex, figuring he'd empathize since he was also in the industry, but his reaction was unexpectedly cold.

"Yeah, yeah. First world problems. You should be grateful you're getting that much work—or any work, really. Do you have any idea how many people would kill to be in your position?" he'd scoffed.

"There's always another new young talent out there… Times change. People's tastes change. Just because you write something good, that doesn't mean people are going to like it. Work takes up all my time, and I still don't feel like a pro, even now. Before I start writing, I'm always terrified. My hands go cold and numb. I'm like, 'Okay, I accepted the job, but can I even do it? Will the producer like it? What about the director?'"

Aguri hadn't planned on telling Yoshioka any of this, but the words naturally slipped off her tongue, as if something about him teased them out of her.

"I believe it. Bet your hands are cold even now. Breaks my heart seein' you like this." Yoshioka's words were tender, soothing. "You've got nobody to warm you up…just like me."

"What about your wife?"

"We split up. I got a daughter who I go see from time to time, though. Cutest li'l girl in the whole world. Think you could use one of your connections to get her in a commercial or somethin'? I'd love to see my little girl's face on the TV," Yoshioka said absent-mindedly. "She's gonna be so beautiful when she grows up. She's four now… Says the cutest darn things, too. 'Daddy, I want you to be happy no matter where you go. And don't forget about me, okay, Daddy?' Isn't she a sweetie?"

Aguri watched in a daze as Yoshioka wiped away his tears with his thick, calloused fingers.

Stop it, Aguri. Her emotions were getting the better of her. *You know what—Yoshioka's tears are contagious. The second he starts crying, it makes me want to cry, too,* Aguri thought as tears welled in her eyes.

"Maybe you heard by now, but…," Yoshioka said as he pushed his glasses back up, "…I bankrupted my father's factory. Tried my hand in all sorts of different trades after that, but none of 'em went anywhere. I'm just a loser."

"…"

"The more I struggled, the worse it got…and I ended up losin' my house, and then my wife left me and took my daughter. I'm helpin' a friend out with a job right now…and one day—this might be a pipe dream, but one day, I wanna get my daughter back."

"Where do you live now?"

"Amagasaki."

"How's the job going?"

Aguri's voice grew quieter. She had no idea what to do, seeing Yoshioka so upset. She wanted the old Yoshioka, the goofball who bragged that his wife-to-be was "a real beauty." The man she practically felt like murdering, the guy she couldn't bring herself to hate, the thoughtless simplicity of his that made her give in. She wanted him to be the same laid-back man he once was.

"Of course, I messed up. Can't deny that. But see, there was no way to recover after the oil crisis... I did everything I could, and still..."

"Men have it rough, too." Aguri genuinely believed that. "You've been through a lot, Yoshioka. You did your best."

Life was hard, regardless of gender.

"There was nothing you could do. You take whatever life throws at you, but sometimes, things just don't work out..."

"Thanks. You're the only one who says anything that nice to me. Well, you and my daughter. But I'm not gonna let it end like this."

Yoshioka interlaced his fingers and stared hard at a fixed point on the floor as he sank into thought.

Aguri dumped out Yoshioka's lukewarm tea and poured him a fresh cup. She always kept the kettle nearby so she wouldn't have to get out of her chair during work meetings. Not even the fragrant aroma of roasted green tea could break Yoshioka out of his trance.

Aguri wondered what would have happened if she'd been there for him. She wondered if she'd helped Yoshioka during his struggles, then maybe he would've been able to rise above adversity. Perhaps dedicating her entire life to him would've been more fulfilling than the empty success she had now.

That made Aguri start to feel that it wasn't Yoshioka who'd abandoned her—she had abandoned him. Like a rat escaping a sinking ship, her ruthless intuition had probably pushed her to cut ties with him before it was too late.

It was hard seeing the man Yoshioka had become. Perhaps he was going to hit Aguri up for some money, and Aguri knew she wasn't going to be able to refuse, because her emotions had gotten the best of her. She justified her quiet despair by telling herself that sacrificing some of her funds would be worth it if it made Yoshioka smile.

Yoshioka suddenly lifted his head back up, a pained expression on his face.

"Aguri...," he started. Aguri nodded repeatedly as if to tell him, *It's okay.*

Money was very important to women who worked in extremely competitive, cutthroat environments, although Aguri didn't feel that way personally. She'd much rather give in and make sacrifices for this poor soul.

"Yes?" Aguri spoke in the gentlest voice she had ever mustered (at least she thought so) in order to make it easier for Yoshioka to open up to her.

"Going bankrupt is, well—it's rough. Day in and day out, I got creditors comin' over, yellin' at me... You go through hell like that, and you quickly learn how to put up with a lot of bullshit."

Aguri remained silent, taken aback by the strange turn the story had taken. That was when Yoshioka let the floodgates open.

"My factory got scammed. Not somethin' ya see every day."

"..."

"Some kinda fraudulent scheme, I guess you could say. Anyway, I reckon it's a pretty rare case, so I was wondering if it'd make a good TV show."

"A show?" Aguri looked at Yoshioka, mouth agape.

"Think maybe you could ask some TV network about it? I've got all the documents and materials you'd need. I'll show 'em to ya."

"..."

"Wouldn't mind writing it myself if you could at least teach me how to write, but...ya know what they say: 'Leave it to the experts.' The story wouldn't have that extra oomph if you didn't write it."

Yoshioka laughed, and his forehead creased like a monkey's once more. He kept switching between *you* and *ya*, most likely without realizing.

Aguri had no idea how to respond. The first thing that came to mind was Yoshioka's motive: Was he planning on turning the bankruptcy into a TV show and winning over the general public as revenge against the person (who Yoshioka claimed was a scam art-ist) responsible for his company's demise?

"What are you looking for in a show about bankruptcy?"

"Anything, really. I just figured I'd take this story to a TV net-work and they'd pay me royalties for it or somethin'." Yoshioka appeared to honestly believe that. "Or you could buy the rights from me."

"I don't really write legal dramas."

Aguri said this so matter-of-factly that she probably sounded cold and distant. However, Yoshioka continued, "How 'bout any of your TV writer friends? Think they'd be interested?"

"Um, well...I guess I could ask."

"Royalty deals pay big money, right? Think you could talk to some movie studios for me, too?"

Aguri had now lost any remaining interest in Yoshioka. She couldn't believe that she was ever in love with the man in front of her, no matter how long ago that was.

But something about Yoshioka tugged at her heartstrings. She had no idea what to do about it, though. She wanted him to be successful and go back to being the childlike, thoughtless man who would break her heart. She never wanted to see him like this.

Aguri grew thirsty and went to take a sip of her tea, but it was too hot to drink. Her unquenchable thirst only added to her mounting frustration.

I Always Had a Feeling

Kozue had been panicking for the past month.

How should she approach him?

Where should she look?

How should she act?

She grew despondent, and her blood was boiling—but not from hatred, which was far too simple a word for what she was feeling. This was a buildup of various emotions. Kozue felt as if she had a bunch of poisons in her gut that a Bunsen burner was slowly bringing to a boil.

But you'd never know that from looking at her. Kozue had to act normal, although she'd forgotten what a normal expression looked like.

Oh, right. Sunglasses. I'll just put on my sunglasses. That way, he can't see my eyes when I look at him, thought Kozue. *That's it. I'll just look at him through some sunglasses!*

She formed circles with her fingers, which she held in front of her eyes like a pair of glasses. She looked left and right, then broke into a toothy smile just like she did when greeting the neighbors.

Kozue then peered into the hand mirror lying on her desk and stared at her reflection. She did a lot of things while she was alone in her room. It was a childhood habit that stuck with her even now at age twenty-eight. She would talk to herself, do impersonations...

"You moron!"

...and secretly call people names. Sometimes, her gestures were meaningless. She would even karate chop the air...

"Hiiiyah!"

...and add sound effects like she was cutting someone down. Somehow, that always left her feeling refreshed. No one in her family knew she did any of this.

When she read a book and tears started to well in her eyes, curiosity would occasionally get the best of her.

I wonder what my face looks like when I'm crying.

Then she'd gaze into her hand mirror, staring hard at each tear escaping the corners of her eyes. She would even forget about whatever had happened in the book she was reading and start crying again because of how pathetic she looked.

Sometimes, the tears flowed when she listened to tapes on her cassette player. Kozue was the kind of woman who would lean against her bookcase on her knees and wipe her tears, wondering, *Do I look pretty right now? Is my stomach sticking out?* while looking down at her belly and sucking it in, then squeezing her rolls.

If only I wasn't like this...

She was still doing the same things at age twenty-eight that she'd done in middle school. Kozue did a lot of different things when she was alone, but she acted totally normal whenever she was in public or with her family (her family being her mother and sister, since her father had passed away three years ago). She worked hard to come across as a well-rounded young woman, and she felt she'd been pulling it off somehow.

That is, until one month ago.

"Kozue, I'm getting married," her younger sister, Midori, had suddenly announced at the dinner table. That was when Kozue's life came crashing down, to put it dramatically.

Midori was twenty-six and worked as a designer for a line of high-end women's clothing at a department store in Osaka. She used to talk about her dreams of spinsterhood and having her own store, which she was going to call Haute Couture Midori.

That was where she differed from Kozue, who went to a run-of-the-mill junior college and ended up not finding work until an acquaintance of her father got her a job as an office clerk for a company that sold fountain pens. It was a small, family-friendly enterprise, and although it was a pleasant job, the pay left much to be desired. Several young men worked there as well, but they were usually out all day meeting clients. For the most part, Kozue was left alone in the office with the elderly accounting manager and another man, who seemed to be a department head. Nonetheless, she'd been at this job for seven or eight years already.

I want to get married one day, Kozue thought as the years went on. *I'm still a kid at heart, though.*

She figured she knew exactly who she was. She liked the idea of getting married but had never really acted on it. That might be cause for concern to some parents, but Kozue's father had passed away, and her mother was now working part-time, so the days simply continued to pass idly by. And yet the thought kept vaguely surfacing:

I'm definitely gonna get married one day.

Her mother was never especially strict about these things, but marriage was a major milestone, so as inexperienced as Kozue was, that seemed like the natural course of action to her. She figured her real life was going to start when she got married, which was why she never expected to be working at this small company for another seven or eight years.

But still, Kozue didn't feel like she'd been single for all that long. In her mind, only two or three years had passed since she'd graduated college. There was never a shortage of young men at her workplace, yet for some reason, they seemed to be getting younger by the year. And when she talked to them about the most recent trends, like music or movies…

"Man, that's so old. That was popular, like, four or five years ago."

…they turned out to be not so recent, after all.

Hmm… Guess I am getting old, Kozue thought. *I'm twenty-eight now.*

That made her ponder things more seriously. But whenever she tried to get serious, her mind ended up high in the clouds, gently floating skyward like a balloon whose string had been cut.

She would look at wedding dresses featured in fashion magazines and daydream.

"I like the frilly collar on this one and the sleeves on that one."

I'm never gonna meet any young guys at this job. Too many old men. I've gotta do something, Kozue thought time after time, but that was nothing more than a fantasy. Diligent as she was, Kozue got up every morning and headed to work as if her fate was set in stone. The company was located in Shinsaibashi on the south side of Osaka, so working in such a lively part of the city was enough to make Kozue happy. And whenever she saw a good-looking guy, she would naturally imagine their marriage and everything that followed. Yet the thought of talking to any of them never once crossed her mind.

Even if her relatives moved on—even if she lost touch with them—even if there were two spinsters in the family, no one would bother to set Kozue up with a man.

Kozue's mother didn't seem to have the energy to worry about Kozue getting married anymore, either. She'd already used half her husband's retirement money to remodel the house.

"I'll just rent out the second floor. Between that and my pension, I should be able to manage on my own."

She was focused on her own post-retirement stability, when Kozue and Midori would be out of the nest. Their mother was optimistic in that sense, convinced that both of them would get married by then. Perhaps Kozue thought along the same lines.

She was childlike in nature, which might explain why people always thought she was younger. That was her only redeeming feature. Men never approached her, maybe because she lacked sex appeal.

Kozue had a round forehead and full, pale cheeks. Below her small, downturned eyes were thin lips and a tiny nose. Her thick neck was also very pale, and her hands were still dimpled. She was plump in every sense of the word. The elderly accounting manager at her job would tell her she was beautiful, but Kozue always thought she looked like one of those *otafuku* masks—in other words, very plain. But she was used to her looks, and there wasn't any part of her that she hated. Kozue was proud of her smooth, glowing skin and liked it very much, but if there was one thing she could change, she'd have higher-set eyes. She looked at herself in her hand mirror and decided she might as well get double-eyelid surgery. Kozue thought she could get it over and done with if she just went to a plastic surgeon, but she lacked the determination to follow through on it. However, Kozue never felt that was a bad thing.

I'd be even prettier if I got the surgery, though…

She continued to simply daydream about the procedure. She knew she needed to do more than that, but the idea got wedged in the back of her mind along with her dreams of plastic surgery and marriage.

Nonetheless, Kozue wanted to devote herself to someone she loved, and that desire grew stronger each year. Perhaps she should've never dreamed so big and instead made the same decision that Midori had:

"I'll never get married. I live for my job."

However, Kozue lacked any real goals or passions. All she had was the hope of one day getting married.

Midori, meanwhile, graduated from high school, then attended a vocational school for dressmaking and even studied in Tokyo. By the time she returned home two years later, she'd become much more stylish and beautiful. She started working in the high fashion industry at a department store in Osaka and polished her skills further. Kozue was convinced that Midori would maintain her vow to never marry, but then all of a sudden, Midori turned her back on her own principle and announced her engagement.

Their mother had been in the bath and not at the table with them.

"Did you tell Mom?" Kozue asked.

"Yeah. I mean, why not?"

Midori's skin was supple and lightly tanned. Being in her line of business meant she was always watching her figure, so she was extremely fit. Her hair was styled in a perfectly straight bob, and her eyes were glistening.

"You don't want people calling us the Spinster Sisters, right? So I figured at least one of us should get married."

"Yeah, makes sense. What's this guy like?"

"Just your average white-collar worker. He's a friend of a friend. We went mountain climbing together."

Now that she mentioned it, Midori did enjoy mountain climbing and often went whenever she had a day off. Kozue, on the other hand, hated walking in general.

"You sure love climbing mountains…"

And she never even toyed with the idea of doing the same.

Kozue liked to cook, so she often packed Midori a lunch before she went to work. Whenever Midori would say, "I'm going to take the first train to work today," Kozue would reply, "Awesome," and get up at four in the morning to cheerfully put some food together. She never felt that cooking for her sister was a burden. If anything, devoting herself to someone else was Kozue's hobby. That was how much she liked helping people. Ever since their mother started working, Kozue had taken over a lot of the household chores. She used the plates and small bowls she got from her monthly subscription, which she paid for herself, to try out various different recipes because she believed it would come in handy whenever she married.

I'm gonna use this one day in my new home, she thought while cooking and arranging dishes as if this were some sort of rehearsal. Kozue tended to live in her own fantasy world, which was why she never felt any urgency to get hitched.

One day when Midori came home late after going out for some drinks, Kozue decided to make her some *ochazuke*. The next moment, she was struck with an idea. She warmed up some rice in the microwave, gently scooped it into a bowl, salted it, and gave it a dash of powdered green tea. Now it was green tea *ochazuke*. She then placed a few lightly salted cucumbers on top. There was nothing like having this year's high-quality green tea from Uji over tender rice mixed with *shiso*. And when you added a cup of fragrant *hojicha* to the mix...

"Kozue, this is seriously delicious. You always make the best food, and I'm not saying that just to be nice," Midori had told her with the biggest smile. That alone was enough to make Kozue happy. It didn't take much for her to be content in life: a face powder that left her skin feeling smooth, wearing new shoes outside on a sunny day, or getting complimented on her green tea *ochazuke*.

"I'm kinda worried, since I can't cook like you."

"Don't let it bother you. You're busy with work. Let me handle things around the house."

That was when Midori said, "Kozue, I'm getting married."

"Whoa, really? I had no idea."

The phrase *getting married* caused Kozue's heart to begin violently racing, even though she wasn't the bride-to-be. It was hard to believe that this was happening to someone close to her.

"Yeah, I was hesitant, to be honest. And I felt kind of guilty getting married before you. But he said he was fine with me still working after we got hitched."

"Who's 'he'?"

"My partner."

Midori apparently referred to her fiancé as her "partner," which was a little ambiguous at times but had a friendly ring to it. Hearing the word *partner* was the final blow, stunning Kozue into complete silence.

Kozue didn't quite feel jealous or inferior—she was just shocked. Marriage, something she dreamed about every day, suddenly struck her like lightning. And it wasn't just anyone's marriage. This was her sister.

"Are you mad?" Midori asked while gripping the knees of her cotton pants.

"Why would I be? This is wonderful news."

"I'll bring my partner over next time. He's a good guy."

Kozue wanted to know where she found this "good guy." She and her sister were relatively close, but they didn't spend as much time together as they used to before Midori left for Tokyo. Midori was very mature for her age, almost as if she were the older sister. Just like Kozue hid the fact that she fantasized about marriage every day, Midori didn't go into detail about her private life, either. They'd created some distance between them, which was probably why they didn't fight anymore despite living together. Midori knew her sister was a dreamer and found it somewhat uncomfortable, which Kozue was well aware of. Whether she knew it or not, Kozue depended on Midori.

Twenty-six-year-old Midori was much more sophisticated than her older sister. But when it came to personal taste, Kozue had to have it her way. She loved frilly fabrics and poufy dresses. Midori's professional side would take over and she'd be on the verge of critiquing her sister's outfit. It was times like this when Kozue chose not to heed an expert's opinion.

"No, this is perfect," Kozue would claim, taking a firm stand in her fluffy blouse and pleated skirt, ready to go out on the town. She wanted tons of pretty, whimsical clothes, regardless of how cheap they were. Midori, on the other hand, had just a few high-quality articles of clothing. Kozue only needed to see something once to fall in love and immediately buy it and put it on, even if it was way too tight. It bothered Midori so much that she would undo the stitches and sew the piece back together without Kozue's permission.

Midori designed clothes that sold for five to six thousand yen each (three thousand for the cheapest stuff). One day, she made an offhanded comment about Kozue's dress.

"Geez, that fabric is paper-thin," she said with a laugh. She didn't mean to be rude, though. She was just a bit shocked that there was actually someone out there who would buy such a whimsical dress. That was her way of showing interest in what her sister was wearing. Nevertheless, Kozue was devastated.

"This dress is fine. There's nothing wrong with it," Kozue insisted, annoyed. After that, she refused to let anyone insult the things she liked anymore. She felt like she was being mocked. Maybe part of the reason was that Midori had career goals she was steadily achieving, which gave Kozue an inferiority complex.

This may not look stylish to a pro, but I like it, Kozue insisted. *Just because she's my little sister doesn't mean we have to like all the same things.*

She was probably being defensive in an unconscious effort to maintain her dignity—the dignity of someone who was extremely sensitive.

"You're right, Kozue. That looks good on you. Cutesy dresses like that actually suit you really well," Midori admitted. "Different strokes for different folks."

Midori was sharp like that. She knew when to back down, even if she didn't necessarily agree. Kozue thought Midori was just humoring her, but it nonetheless made her feel instantly better.

She'd gotten complacent living in an all-female household and being complimented on her food and clothing. The days kept on passing her by. Kozue's family lived in bare-bones municipal housing built right after the Second World War. The city had sold these houses for a bargain around the time Kozue's parents got married, so everyone on the block was fortunate enough to have their own property. Plus, being in the suburbs of Osaka was extremely convenient. The houses weren't very big, but they'd all been rebuilt in the '50s and '60s and eventually added additional floors. Kozue's house had been remodeled three times, and after her father passed away, they'd decided to add a second floor with two eight-square-meter rooms, one for each sister.

Kozue was comfortable with her tiny personal space because she believed that one day, she would get married and move out. The dream alone was enough to fulfill her year after year. There was a sliding door that divided her room and Midori's, and sometimes, they opened it during hot summers and slept side by side. Kozue enjoyed this peaceful, cozy lifestyle, although perhaps Midori didn't share the sentiment.

"Sis, can you not open my drawers whenever you feel like it?"

Midori had been smiling when she said that, but her tone was firm. Kozue shared a dresser with her mother on the first floor, and Midori had brought a dresser with her when she moved back from Tokyo and placed it against the wall. Kozue had opened one of the drawers.

"Sorry. I just wanted to borrow a pad."

Kozue had seen Midori put menstrual pads in that drawer before, so she'd gone ahead and opened it.

"There's plenty of pads downstairs in the bathroom," Midori grumbled.

Kozue immediately shrank back whenever her sister got mad at her, but she could never retort with something like *What's your problem?!* Instead, she always felt bad, like she'd messed up somehow. She knew very well that her sister was more mature than her, so she blamed herself entirely. She figured that if Midori was that angry, then she must have done something very wrong. And yet...

She didn't have get that angry. All I did was open a stupid drawer.

Kozue didn't keep a journal, but she had a feeling that Midori kept one of her own, not that she would ever sneak a peek. But one day, she secretly opened Midori's dresser drawer when she wasn't home. Folded inside were handkerchiefs and scarves, with a box of sanitary napkins in the back, and under that was a thin box she had never seen before. Kozue inspected it closely and pulled out the slim, rubber item inside.

Her inherent curiosity got the better of her, and she stared at the object. *Is this what I think it is?* She couldn't help but feel it was much smaller and thinner than she'd imagined.

Kozue figured that maybe girls nowadays saw or even owned one of these starting in middle school.

Oh man. This is wild.

She immediately put the item away in a panic.

Kozue had read about these in magazines before, but this was her first time actually seeing one in person—one owned by someone she was close to, no less. She was getting worked up, so she went back to her room and started karate chopping the air.

"Hiiiyah!" she shouted, then added, "Phew, that thartled me..." and grabbed her hand mirror, wondering what kind of face she was making.

When Kozue was a child, she couldn't pronounce *startled* correctly. Her father thought it was so cute and used to copy her. Soon, everyone in the family started saying "that thartled me" when they were in a good mood. Kozue hadn't even thought about that old habit until it slipped off her tongue.

Kozue wondered if Midori ever got the chance to use this thing, and if she did, that made her way more of an adult than Kozue herself. While Kozue had read a lot on the subject, she had absolutely no experience to go along with it, so the whole thing was still somewhat shrouded in mystery. She could certainly imagine the heated passion involved, although she didn't understand it enough to put it into words.

Kozue felt as if she were covered in a thick fog as she idly dreamed her life away. Perhaps karate chopping the air and shouting "Hiiiyah!" was her unconscious way of trying to get rid of that fog.

When Midori told her she was getting married, Kozue immediately remembered what she'd found in her sister's drawer.

Guess people who get married are just on a different level, Kozue thought, as if that didn't apply to her.

She knew nothing about Midori's marriage—or even marriage in general, really—until it actually happened.

Midori introduced her fiancé to her mother first, at her mother's workplace. That was very typical of Midori. Apparently, her fiancé was a year younger than her.

"He was so tall. Seemed to be in good shape, too. Looked a bit like a lumberjack, but still really sweet." Their mother had apparently taken an interest in him.

"Hmm. A lumberjack, huh?" Kozue replied.

Then she started fantasizing about her mother setting her up with that young man. That was why Kozue had been so restless at the office. But it was all a mere fantasy, of course. Kozue felt as if her imagination was constantly slapping her in the face.

Her paternal aunt in Kyoto brought some wedding money over as a gift to congratulate Midori.

"Hey, Kozue. You must be jealous, huh? But your time will come. I'm sure you'll find the perfect man for you, so don't get jealous. Just be happy for your little sister."

She was trying to cheer Kozue up, but what she said was still enough to annoy even someone as good-natured as Kozue.

"I never said I was jealous. How rude," she replied.

This was what made her blood boil. It wasn't hatred or envy. She felt all sorts of emotions, naturally: inferiority, despair, resentment, melancholy, gloom, and loneliness. But it wasn't all negative feelings; she was also giddy and curious. It was like how a beautifully colored marble shone even brighter while mixed with dark-colored marbles. These emotions were like beautiful poisons bubbling in a flask. Kozue was anxious but enjoying the sensation. And then her aunt's strange attempt at sympathy made Kozue feel like someone had lit a Bunsen burner, boiling the poisons inside her until *BOOM!* they exploded.

Kozue went to her room on the second floor.

"You moron!" she hissed while karate chopping the air. "Hiiiyah!"

Even her neighbors wouldn't give her a break. Many of them had lived in the area for decades.

"Your sister's getting married, I hear? I bet you'll miss her when she moves out."

All the marriage talk started to take over the conversation at home as well: who had introduced the couple, how Midori was going to make her own wedding dress because she didn't want or like the rental dresses, how they were going to live in an apartment in southern Osaka, and when the two families were going to meet. Midori already had everything perfectly planned out. Their mother was indecisive (just like Kozue), so her only response was, "Oh, that's nice."

"We both paid for the apartment's deposit with our savings, so we're gonna be living paycheck to paycheck for a while. That's why I'll be taking some of the old dishes and spoons with me," said Midori. "Doesn't matter how many there are or if they don't all match. It's not like I can really cook anything special anyway. My partner's a way better cook. He always cooks when we go to the mountains."

"Oh, does he?"

An absurd scene popped into Kozue's head of a giant lumberjack cooking in the kitchen, and her heart started racing as if he were cooking for her.

When she went to work, she would tell anyone she could, "My sister is getting married," as if she herself had achieved a feat, but when someone told her, "You better hurry up and get married, too. You need to keep up with your sister," she found herself annoyed, even though this was a consequence of her own actions. On the whole, however, Kozue was just half-annoyed; the other half was excited. She spent her days in bliss as if she were the one who was getting married. While her neighbors', coworkers', and aunt's responses bothered her, there was something curious her mother said that really got her attention.

"Now that I think about it, I remember seeing a lot of mail from that Kawagoe guy."

"Like letters? For Midori?"

"Yeah, there were times he was sending around three a week, even."

"Seriously? I had no idea."

In Kozue's household, her mother was always the first to get home from work, so she would always be the first to check the mail. She would then place mail for her daughters in each of their rooms on the second floor, which was why Kozue had no idea her sister was getting so many letters.

She felt genuine envy when she first heard about the letters.

What's so important that he needed to write three letters a week to say?

When she thought about it even more, Kozue became confused and disgusted. Midori started looking more and more like an intimidating grown-up woman, receiving all these correspondences from a man without saying a peep about it. Meanwhile, Midori continued to compliment Kozue.

"This food you cooked is seriously delicious."

Then she started trying on the wedding dress she'd made. "It's finished. What do you think?"

The simple white satin dress looked perfect on Midori's tall, slim figure. It was a piece meant for mature, adult women, but Kozue still felt incredibly envious. Perhaps for a dreamer like her, actually seeing something in real life awakened her jealous impulses, unlike when that same something was still but an abstract idea. Nevertheless, Kozue wanted to maintain her dignity, so she'd never let anyone find that out. She was probably annoyed by what her aunt said because there was an element of truth to it.

Kozue wanted to wear her sunglasses because she wanted to hide how flustered she was.

"He's coming over this Sunday," Midori said, which only distressed Kozue even more. "You should check him out."

She sounded as if she was talking about an object. She said she'd bring him over, have him meet Kozue, and then they'd have tea with their mother.

"Why not have him stay for dinner? I could cook something up,"

Kozue fervently suggested. Just knowing that man was coming over made her giddy with excitement. Thinking about what to cook for him made her happy.

"Really? You'd do that for us?"

Midori's smile made her look like she was reading Kozue like a book, although perhaps that was Kozue's negative skepticism at work.

Midori never spent the night at her fiancé's place, but ever since she announced their engagement, she'd started coming home even later than usual. She returned in the middle of the night when Kozue was already asleep, using her spare key to get in before climbing to the second floor and heaving a sigh of relief.

"Phew…"

A strong, exotic odor filled the air, perhaps the smell of foreign liquor or perfume. Midori turned on her bedside lamp and started getting undressed. Kozue was usually the one to lay out the futons, since the closet was in her room. Midori was sloppily removing her clothes; maybe she was drunk. She pulled off her light-purple panty-hose and practically tossed them into Kozue's room. The stench of perfume, liquor, and foreign cigarettes permeated the air, so potent it seemed like something that mature women exuded from their very pores. Midori exhaled again.

"Phew…!"

Kozue thought it sounded like Midori's pantyhose had sighed.

Silence ensued, so she gently turned her head to see what was happening. Midori had tossed her suit and bra onto the floor and was fast asleep on her futon. She was wearing only the top half of her pajamas, as if she got annoyed and gave up putting on the rest. Her thin white cotton panties looked no different from a tiny bikini, and a shock of glossy hair conspicuously peeked through from underneath. Midori had her lower half splayed out across the futon. Her smooth, tanned legs looked muscular and athletic, and the tufts of hair that framed her groin were just as conspicuous as the rest of it. Midori and her pubic hair were similarly shameless. Kozue flinched as if she had been punched in the nose.

It was a stark reminder that she had nothing on an adult woman.

The weather that Sunday was sunny and hot, marking the first real day of summer. The beaches were open for swimming and mountains for climbing, although it rained on and off for the next few days or so.

Midori returned home with her fiancé Sunday night before it got dark. Kozue had cooked a seemingly random assortment of dishes. Egg foo young, salt-grilled sweetfish, pumpkin soup—it was a smorgasbord of Chinese, Japanese, and Western cuisines, and she worried how they might take it. She had high expectations for this fiancé, which was why she was doubting herself and thinking maybe she should have gone with something that had a little more punch to it. This was their first time hosting a young man for dinner, and the anxiety was making her head spin.

It was a little past six thirty, the agreed upon time, when Kozue heard Midori's voice. She rushed out of the kitchen in a panic and sprinted straight for the bathroom in the back. They had turned a small yard into a bathroom when they remodeled the place, so the vanity was in the hall. Kozue hurriedly put on her makeup and ended up using far more face powder than usual. She felt like her lipstick was too deep a shade of red as well.

She grinned in the mirror out of habit to see how she would look smiling, but this time, her heart was pounding as she wondered how this Mr. Kawagoe—this partner—this lumberjack would see her.

"Over here?" came a man's voice as the glass door to the hallway slid open. The bathroom was right next to the tub.

He honestly looked like an alien to her. He was tan and much taller than she'd expected. Kozue's startled face as she stood in front of the vanity took him by surprise.

"Pardon me," he said with a bow of his head. Kozue ran past him, escaping into the kitchen while smiling through her tears. After the man finished his business, he left the bathroom and went into the living room. Kozue heard him talking to their mother.

"Sis, will you come out already? You thartled me. Are you being shy or something?" Midori called before turning to the young man. "She's a little shy," she told him, smiling.

"She's just like me, then. Glad I get to meet someone I can relate to," he replied nonchalantly.

Kozue hadn't noticed his masculine, chiseled features moments ago in the hallway. They perfectly matched his cheerful voice.

"Hurry up, Kozue. Come on, get over here, you silly goose," Midori teased. Then their mother started chuckling. Kozue was far too embarrassed to come out now. She'd always been interested in men like this one, and she felt as if she had been waiting for someone like him her entire life. His young energy was phenomenal, as if he had brought life to this little old house. Blood rushed to Kozue's dizzy head.

But this man was her sister's fiancé.

Perhaps the dreamer Kozue would simply continue dreaming until she drew her last breath, never to meet such a man.

Kozue always had a feeling that would happen, and yet there was nothing she could do about it.

"You're so funny, Sis. Hurry up and get over here."

"Hmph," Kozue mumbled weakly as she prepared to carry dinner into the living room.

This was just who she was. Maybe when she stepped foot into the living room, she'd ramble on and on, unable to stop herself from getting excited. She could even imagine herself doing that in a past life.

Love's Coffin

It's fine if Yuuji comes. If he doesn't, that's fine, too, Une thought.

Une had no interest in forcing things to happen. She always went with the flow. Nevertheless, she still believed he would come, no matter what. Perhaps Yuuji hadn't realized it yet, but he was like a loyal dog who followed Une wherever she went.

I'm always so rude with my comparisons...

She laughed to herself.

Une didn't look like a mean person on the outside. She was wearing a thick blue-gray cotton suit, perfect for late summer, and a straw hat in hand. She was average height but looked tall because of her good posture. She had bushy brownish hair that was naturally a shade lighter than most and fair skin to match. Freckles appeared on her cheeks whenever she got a tan, making her look more domestic than anything else. Une always had the subtlest of smiles on her face, and her eyes held a quiet strength.

But it wasn't easy to pick up on her strong-willed, sadistic intentions. Even Yuuji believed she was nothing more than his sweet, friendly aunt who never got mad at him when he needed attention.

That was why he always wanted to be around her, never realizing that the real reason was because he was attracted to her sexually.

Une thought he was like a dog drawn to an enticing smell he couldn't get enough of.

All that being said, it wasn't like Une hated Yuuji. In fact, she found him to be very likable. She had both a loving and a cold side to her. She adored this nineteen-year-old, but at the same time, she loved picking on him as well. She was always laughing at him deep down whenever he came to her as if he was expecting or wanting something. And yet he was the apple of her eye.

"Yuuji, have you ever even kissed a girl before?"

That was the kind of question she liked to tease him with.

"I have," he defensively replied. "In elementary school."

"That was forever ago. What about recently?"

"Why do you care? If you think I'm lying, then how about we try so you can see for yourself?"

"Adults kiss differently than kids. You wouldn't be able to handle it."

"Dammit. You're just making fun of me, aren't you?"

"Don't worry. We can give it a try one day when you're ready."

"Yeah, yeah! You wish!"

Would Yuuji come to the hotel at Mount Rokko?

Une decided to go to Mount Rokko by car. She figured she could savor the drive along the way, then enjoy a relaxing four-to-five-day vacation and wear several new outfits, which was why she had packed a lot in her suitcase. Une used her car for work as well, so she always kept a spare pair of shoes and an easy-to-slip-on sweater inside. She'd had this little red vehicle for many years now and had grown accustomed to it. Une loved that tiny car; she called it her music box.

Her apartment's garage was on the basement level, so when the elevator finally came, it was already completely full with mothers and their children. Summer vacation had started four or five days ago, and it seemed that kids who were in kindergarten were on break as well. The children were talking their little yellow hats off while the mothers were conversing among themselves. Une was apathetic about children (and of course, their mothers), and while she would greet them with a nod since they were neighbors, she would never say a word to them.

After they got off at the first floor, the kids scattered, filling up the lobby as they ran around. There were far more than a few people with small children living in this apartment complex, and it was like they had tunnel vision when it came to their kids. Une was almost knocked over and trampled on, simply for being on the first floor at the wrong time. It was as if the children's parents couldn't even see her.

Une believed there was something very egotistical about having kids—an opinion she wouldn't dare speak aloud. The twenty-nine-year-old never said more than needed to be said. Nor did she let any extraneous feelings show on her face. As the elevator descended, she thought about how annoying and awful children were, but she wouldn't breathe a single word of it. She simply held her tongue with an emotionless expression.

She wasn't that way at work, though. She had spent the past seven years working at a furniture store that sold products using textiles made by a major company. She was an interior designer who provided consultations to customers, showing them samples and providing price quotes. Remodeling apartments was also a big part of her work. She would carry around a large sample book (hence why Une was pretty strong) along with a catalogue of door-knobs, light fixtures, chairs, and tables to show the customers. Sometimes these endless consultations touched on household topics like family living and personal preferences, in which cases Une always came across as good with children.

"Hey, little guy. How old are you? What's your name?" she would say, bending over to meet the child's eye. It came more or less naturally to her, and she didn't hate it, either. She didn't talk to her customers' kids because she was trying to put on a show for their parents. She was genuinely curious about them, which surprised even her. Perhaps it was an aftereffect of being so keyed up at work, which required her to be aggressive and competitive. Whenever she put in the effort, she was very approachable, cheerful, and dependable, which was why many customers would ask for her by name. She had a very natural and charming affect to her when she said things like, "Hey, little guy. How old are you? We're gonna make you the coolest room in the whole world."

I guess that means..., Une vaguely thought as she started up the car, *...I really do have a split personality.*

Her ex-husband had told her she had a split personality to insult her during their divorce four years ago, but now she found the humor in his comment and even admitted it wasn't totally off the mark.

He's got a point. I can't blame him. Both personalities are the real me.

Sakimura, her ex, had once pointed out that she acted and looked completely different when she was talking to him compared to his mother. She hadn't thought about it until he brought it up, but she more or less agreed. They used to live with his mother when they were married, and Une would always do her best to be smiling and cheerful around her mother-in-law to get her to like her.

Meanwhile, Une was completely herself with her husband. She would say exactly what was on her mind and make it obvious when she was bored or not in a good mood. Une wasn't exactly worried about whether she really did have a split personality. She was more taken aback by the weight of the words.

"You're always so rude to me when we're fighting, but the second my mom calls for you, you turn into a different person, all smiley and eager to help. Just seeing you like that makes me sick. It's like you have a split personality."

The coldness of his accusation really hurt her. This wasn't a bit of lighthearted banter—it was purely malicious. She could tell that her husband didn't love her. It had finally all made sense. She'd realized what had been bothering her and why their relationship didn't seem to be working. After a year and a half of marriage, Une learned that her husband still hadn't ended a relationship with another woman, which was what led to their divorce.

Une decided to drive through the mountains. Rather than cut straight through town via the highway, she preferred taking the meandering local roads among the foothills, since she enjoyed the fresh air and view. The summertime heat was still in full swing, something she noticed as a warm breeze blew through the car windows, carrying dust along with it. Regardless, this was Une's vacation and hers alone. She didn't need to worry about her hair getting messed up or getting dirty. She just went wherever the wind blew.

Yuuji had been surprised when he showed up at her place last night.

"What are you doing taking a vacation this time of year?"

"I always take time off in September. It's my summer vacation. My boss is totally fine with it. I usually take the end of the year off like everyone else, but I make sure to have my summer break a little later than most."

Watching Une pack piqued Yuuji's curiosity.

"Can I come with you?" he asked.

"You have cram school to go to, don't you? I'm pretty sure your mommy wouldn't want you skipping that."

"Don't give me excuses."

"I booked a really nice hotel. I can't have you waddling around with your basketball shoes on. You have to wear a tie and look nice, or they won't let you in. Kids aren't allowed, either."

"Ah, you gotta be old to get in, huh? Gotcha," Yuuji replied. "So how long are you going to be there?"

"Four or five days."

"Oh wow. I wish I could stay just for a night!"

"I don't want your mom yelling at me over the phone again like last time."

Yuuji started cracking up.

Une was sixteen years younger than her sister. This older sister and her older brother were actually Une's half siblings; Une was the only biological child of her father's second wife. She fell out of contact with her two half siblings when their parents died, and eventually, they grew distant. It didn't help that her older sister was the one who set her up with Sakimura, so drifting apart after things went sour was an inevitability.

They always invited her to her father's memorial, but she wasn't able to make it one year, so her sister's youngest son, Yuuji, went to her place to deliver some of the leftover offerings. Une hadn't seen him since he was in elementary school, so she was startled to discover he was already taller than her. They stared at each other, blushing.

It wouldn't be an exaggeration to say Une fell in love with Yuuji at that moment.

He had failed his college entrance examination and was attending cram school for the time being. Soon, Yuuji started hanging out at Une's place every once in a while.

"Feels like something's pulling me here. Like a magnet."

"And what's the magnet?"

"You, Une."

Yuuji used to not be able to pronounce his aunt's name correctly when he was a kid. Now he was interested in her tidy, compact apartment where she lived alone. Une didn't have any younger siblings and had been raised like an only child, so she enjoyed watching a tall, skinny, baby-faced boy curiously exploring her house.

"Here, listen to this. This album is amazing," he would say when bringing records over. He also borrowed books from time to time, which she didn't mind.

"Wait! Don't touch that! Don't ever open that, okay?"

She even scolded him occasionally. Yuuji took her to a concert once, so she took him to a Kabuki show in return, since he said he had never been before, but he was quiet the entire show.

"I thought I was gonna lose my mind from boredom!" he'd said. "I think the actors were bored, too, save for maybe the leads. The guys playing the side roles seemed like they were enjoying seeing the look on the audience's faces, especially when they noticed someone sleeping. Their expressions were like, 'Yep, I'd be sleeping, too, if I weren't getting paid.'"

That made Une laugh.

Yuuji sometimes stopped by her place with just a binder and some books, and one day, he left them at her place and forgot about them. Une waited for him to come back and get them, but after a month went by and he never came over, she decided to call her older sister and tell her he forgot his stuff. Une's sister had another son and daughter still at home, but she was nonetheless the one who answered when Une called.

"Yeah, I heard Yuuji spent the night at your place the other day," her sister had said.

Une fell silent for a moment but almost immediately replied that that was when he'd left some of his belongings at her place. Yuuji ended up coming over a few days later.

"So where'd you go that night? I can't believe you told your mom you were staying here."

"I was with a girl. It was my first time...if you know what I mean." Yuuji scratched his ear.

"How was it?"

"Not as good as I thought it'd be. I said I liked listening to those late-night programs and letting my imagination run wild. She ended up smacking my ass and telling me to get my act together. Absolutely no respect."

Yuuji made himself at home and started drinking some soda he grabbed out of the refrigerator. Une, meanwhile, was still facing her mirror on the dresser.

"Why would you even sleep with someone so uptight? Are you that desperate?"

"I dunno. I'm sure I'd have had a good time if it was with someone like you, though."

"Hmph."

"I want to be with you."

"Why?"

"I don't know. Maybe 'cause you're different than the others. It's fun talking to you. Way more fun than anything my mom and I ever talk about."

"Well yeah, I'd hope so. I don't nag you about your college entrance exam or your grades, so of course you'd prefer me, you lazy bum."

"No, that's not it, but...whatever."

Une was no different. She never got tired of looking at Yuuji: the clumsy way he used his hands, his lanky legs whenever he casually stretched out on a chair or table, the way his soft black hair brushed against his forehead. Every time he came over on Sunday afternoons, she gave him a warm welcome like any good aunt would. But the moment he took off his shoes with their worn heels at the entrance and the smell of a young man's sweat rose into the air, Une would close the front door, lock it, and chuckle to herself as if she had just trapped her next victim. She had no idea when she started to feel that way. She had a split personality, after all. She would say, "Oh, hey. Come in, Yuuji," while coldly thinking, *You're here again? Go home.*

And she pitied his childlike youth and how he would fall for her kindness, get far too used to it, and indulge himself.

Kindness was nothing more than a facade—a mask worn by adults. It pained Une to see him so naively trusting, oblivious to the disgusting truth that an adult's kindness could change into a threat or blackmail at the drop of a hat. Une kind of understood the solitary pleasure that contemporary European sex offenders felt when they lured innocent children to their deaths with smiles and candy, just like a villain straight out of *Grimms' Fairy Tales*. Every one of them had an elaborate split personality as well.

Une made small talk as she took off her stockings and ran a bath.

"Yuuji, go turn off the water…"

Yuuji immediately got up and went to the bathroom, but hanging out to dry were Une's panties, bra, and stockings. And she knew that. Yuuji returned as if he'd seen nothing special, but there was no way it hadn't attracted his attention.

"Hey, tell me about that girl. The one who smacked your ass," Une said with a laugh as she organized photos for work. She always took pictures of the rooms she was involved in designing and arranging, then sorted them before putting them in an album at home. Yuuji pretended he was distracted by her work and changed the subject.

"Forget her. What about you? Do you have a boyfriend? Show me a pic."

"I don't have a boyfriend, and I wouldn't show you even if I did."

"Huh… My sister shows pics of her boyfriend to basically anyone. And as if that wasn't enough, she even sent some to a magazine that ended up publishing them in this section called 'My Pride and Joy.' She always does that kind of stuff. You're not into that?" Yuuji asked, seemingly distracted by the movement of Une's fingers. She had a slightly dark manicure.

Yuuji would sometimes say "Lemme see that ring" as an excuse to touch her fingers. He slowly grew accustomed to touching her body, until one day, she was brushing her hair when he grabbed the brush.

"Want me to brush the back for you?"

Une found his clumsy movements and shameless yet sheepish expression hilarious.

"Yuuji, have you told your parents that you've been coming over here a lot lately?"

Yuuji replied that he hadn't.

Une went to the bathroom to wash her hands, and while she was watching Yuuji in the mirror, she saw him pick up and smell her powder puff and handkerchief with the lingering scent of her perfume. She knew he was doing this, but she pretended like she didn't notice. Granted, with her split personality, she could've teased him and asked, *What are you doing?* if she wanted to embarrass him. She could have pointed out plenty of perverse things young men did and made him feel so ashamed that he wouldn't even know what to do with himself. She could've been blunt and said, *Why do you come over so often anyway? Expecting me to do something for you? I see that look in your eyes* to startle him.

Just imagining these situations delighted Une. She felt like the old witch who lured Hansel and Gretel into her house in the woods, and she took pleasure in the silly things Yuuji did like secretly smell her belongings, thinking he was being sneaky.

After passing through Mount Kabuto, she was suddenly met with cooler, more refreshing temperatures. Une opened the car window, stopped in a forest of Japanese cedar, and deeply inhaled the fresh mountain air. The nature parks in the area were usually packed during summer vacation, but hers was the only car in sight this time of year.

There wasn't a cloud in the sky when she arrived at the hotel that afternoon on the mountain's summit. Une spent a few days here every year at the beginning of September, and the man at the reception desk remembered her, politely welcoming her in. Hotels in the mountains sometimes underwent remodeling or construction work during the off-season, which could be disappointing, but this place was usually quiet when Une visited. With the chaos of summer already over, this felt like an actual vacation.

Une reserved a twin room every year. Rooms were still at peak season pricing, which was more than she could really afford, but there was no way to put a price on the view. The scenery was beautiful at night, and during the day, she had a sweeping vista of the entire town along the coast with the horizon blurred from all the fog.

There was complete silence, and Une was overwhelmed with a feeling of neither exactly satisfaction nor boredom. She'd had her slightly off-season vacation at this hotel last year and the year before, but nobody ended up coming, much to her disappointment. Not that someone would come, since she never told anyone where she was going. She didn't even have a man she could tell, for starters. She'd gotten to know only two men following her divorce, neither of whom were particularly exciting people to be around. Une believed all men were different, and these two were disposable after she had her fun with them. They'd both worked for her employer's parent company before getting transferred. Une couldn't even remember what they looked like. All of her coworkers—save for her boss—were extremely young. While many men sneaked looks at her while she was at work, she gradually got used to the attention and decided to focus on herself: being the freckled, beautiful woman with a sweet smile who was passionate about her job as an interior designer and good at it, too.

That was why she decided to splurge once a year, when she would book an expensive hotel in the mountains during the off-season. She would eat dinner alone every night. Most people who came to resorts were either couples or families. The only people who would talk to her were basically the bellhop and the manager. Une liked it this way, though. There was a time and place for picking up men at hotels in the city, like when she was riding high on her work successes. But she wanted to stay at this hotel to get away from her job and have some genuine rest and relaxation, which meant staying away from men. The fact that Une was able to take time off during the off-season was proof that she was working hard. And she would pick up men at hotels in the city from time to time when work was going well, which made her both mentally and physically fulfilled.

Une took her clothes out of her suitcase and tossed them on one of the beds, then changed into her white cotton pants and cotton sweater before leaving her room. She decided to go for a walk through the foothills. It was hot outside, but the mountain breeze already had the crisp bite of autumn. The pine trees near the hotel were beautiful and lush, not yet soiled by car exhaust. Une took off her sunglasses and basked in the pine trees and Japanese cedar. After walking straight ahead for a while, she found herself at the Tenguiwa cable railway station. There wasn't a single soul out for a walk like she was, and when she finally reached the station, it had just one employee. It was an extremely lonely sight.

From this high up, Une could see the ocean and city situated among the mountains as well as the exposed mountain peaks. Standing alone at a place like this made her face the days past. She usually didn't get this way until the third or fourth day of her vacation, but this year, she was already feeling incredibly empty the moment she got here. Nevertheless, Une was used to that, and it wasn't painful in the slightest. She was lonely, but she liked being alone; without work on her mind, she could finally relax. And yet she couldn't help but think about the quotes she needed to come up with for her customers when she got home. She imagined how she would tell them that they'd save 20 percent if they used this new, high-quality vinyl wallpaper instead and how she would offer them a new price quote to demonstrate that.

Guess my split personality even comes out when I'm alone, she thought.

It was a foggy night. A fine, misty rain fell on the open-air dining hall, rendering the world completely invisible. Une finished her traditional Japanese meal, then downed an entire bottle of sake by herself. She had a habit of catching up on all the reading she'd been meaning to do during this vacation, so she'd brought four or five books with her, but she was far too tired that night to read.

When she woke up in the middle of the night, the fog had already cleared. A nippy breeze blew outside the window, and both the sky and the earth were bathed in radiant light. It wouldn't be an exaggeration to say that the starlight and the lamplights were violently bright, even. It was absolutely stunning.

After returning to the hotel that afternoon from her walk on her second day of vacation, she found Yuuji awkwardly sitting in the quiet hall, dressed in a suit and a tie. He tried to play it cool.

"Yo," he said with a wave, but he was so nervous that each movement was awkward, and his soft, childlike lips were pulled into a sulking frown. He looked like a kid on the verge of tears, fidgeting and anxious that Une was going to scold him.

Une could have gone either way with this due to her split personality:

What are you doing here? Go home.

Or even…

I'm glad you're here. Enjoy your stay.

However, she used the dangerous weapon she had been secretly carrying with her: kindness.

"You look good. Is that yours?" she asked, nodding at him.

"It's my brother's," he replied. "I didn't tell him I was borrowing it, though. Told my family I was going to an overnight seminar."

It wasn't foggy outside that day. The sky and sea seemed even closer than usual. Back in Une's room, Yuuji stared out the window, seemingly at a loss for words. He'd come with a single duffle bag.

"You must have sweated a lot in that suit. Go take a shower," Une suggested while undoing Yuuji's tie. "Why did you twist this so much? Do you still not know how to tie a tie?" she added. Yuuji's eyes slowly lit up with joy; he must've felt light-headed as a result. He almost looked mad as he pushed Une's hand away.

"Why are you facing that way to take off your clothes?"

Une's teasing voice was full of life and brimming with delight. Yuuji didn't reply. All of a sudden, Une's eyes were briefly met with his naked back, youthfully smooth and beautifully tanned. He still had tan lines from wearing a swimsuit at the beach that summer, so his butt was very white.

When Yuuji came back, the room was faintly dim, since Une had closed the curtains. Yuuji silently walked across the carpet before suddenly stopping.

"Une…," he anxiously called.

"I'm over here." Une was hidden under the sheets, so Yuuji couldn't see her. "Come."

Yuuji was in his underwear.

"I'm leaving," he said.

"Why? Isn't this why you came?"

Une's lips were curling into the smirk of a criminal—her other personality. And she could sense his silent repulsion as well—the repulsion Yuuji felt, full of loathing for this woman who'd made him lose his composure.

"Is this not what you wanted to do?"

Une doubled down and teased him again like the sadist she was. Yuuji was furious and on the verge of losing control. He seemed about to reject Une's attempt to stop him from leaving, but he somehow ended up collapsing onto the bed, on top of her. There was nothing covering her body.

She tried to kiss him, but he was trembling. His teeth were chattering as well.

"I love you," she said to calm him down. "I've always liked you, ever since I first laid eyes on you."

Yuuji seemed to be saying something, too, so she strained her ears.

"Me too." His voice was hoarse. "Ever since I first saw you."

Une was enjoying rubbing the smooth, soft skin of a young man.

Yuuji nervously trembled. Even his fingers were trembling. Une had never felt pleasure like this in her life. No man, not even her ex-husband, ever made her feel like she did at that moment. Pure, undiluted ecstasy flooded every inch of her body before tapering to a point and piercing her from head to toe. Her split personality gradually came into focus until it became one complete personality.

Those words—the insult her husband spited her with—seemed to have wounded Une deeply without her ever even realizing it. But she didn't care anymore.

Yuuji seemed to be dumbfounded, as if he didn't know when it was over. Une changed into a thin white nightgown and opened the curtains to reveal a view of the forest. There weren't any buildings in this direction, so she didn't have to worry about being seen. A breathtaking sunset glow painted the expanse of trees.

Une and Yuuji lay in bed, staring at the crimson sky, and Une said, "This sunset seems to go on forever…"

"To tell the truth…," Yuuji mumbled vacantly, "…this was my first time. I didn't get anywhere with that other girl. All she did was touch me and I—"

"Don't worry about that." Une was serious. "To tell the truth, I really liked it. I've been wanting to do this for so long."

"No way."

Yuuji had a habit of saying that. It was his way of saying "Really?"

"Yes way. I could die happy right now, no regrets."

"I'd rather not die yet. Still gotta work on my game, after all."

Une laughed.

After it grew dark, they got dressed to go eat dinner. Une changed into a black chiffon dress. Yuuji seemed to enjoy his new job of zipping it up and closing the clasp to her diamond pendant.

Une slightly adjusted his tie and checked whether his shoes, which he didn't seem used to wearing, were polished. It was blatantly obvious that he was wearing borrowed clothes, perhaps because of the expression on his face: one of vague superiority mingled with inferiority. Nevertheless, Une leaned into him while wrapping her arm around his, causing him to stagger as they walked, head held high.

The hallway was empty, and no one else was waiting for the elevator. There was a long, narrow window, and the bottom half of it had a clear view of the city's sea of lights. Une stopped before the window.

"Look," she said.

Yuuji gazed in the direction of the lights, but his eyes were welling with tears, and his eyelids were growing puffy. He suddenly moved as if he was going to push her against the wall, but he was so rough and crude about it that it was almost depressing to watch. It wasn't clear why he suddenly wanted to kiss her, but Une understood how he felt and kissed him back. The elevator arrived, and people got off on their floor, so they stepped away from each other and got inside.

They were all alone in the elevator. Une gently wiped Yuuji's lips with a handkerchief. There was a smudge of rouge on them; he looked upset.

Since they had a reservation, the restaurant immediately seated them at a table with a seaside view. The billowing white fog ebbed and flowed with the passage of time, revealing the city lights only to hide them once again. Once they'd finished their fish dinner, the sommelier, whom Une was acquainted with, stopped by their table and asked if they would care for some German wine.

"It's a rare wine from Wiltingen. I'm sure you would love it."

Usually, Une would tell him to bring her whatever, but even conversations like this left an impression on her that night, which she very much enjoyed. She jokingly put on airs and asked:

"What's it called?"

"Scharzhofberger. It was fermented at the Egon Muller estate, which produces the region's best wines. It has a smooth, refreshing taste."

"All right, we'll have some."

The entire exchange was a joy to her. Yuuji hadn't been paying attention to the conversation, and even he seemed to have clammed up. His eyes were glued on Une, but that didn't make her uncomfortable at all. He must have forgotten to take his mystified gaze off her, which she found cute. Une cautiously placed her hand over Yuuji's on the table so nobody would notice.

"Une, you're so beautiful. I remember how beautiful I thought you were when I first saw you and how I couldn't stop blushing," he stammered.

"Me too. I was so red."

"No way. You were always smiling like you wanted to tease me."

"Only because I liked you so much."

"No way?!"

His reaction was very childlike and a sudden reminder to her that this was real. There was no doubt that fireworks were going off in Yuuji's head right now. There was no doubt he had no idea what Egon Muller or Scharzhofberger were, either. Une slowly indulged in the chilled wine while enjoying its apple-like, refreshing taste. Yuuji, on the other hand, was less preoccupied with the fish or wine and was undoubtedly thinking only about the starlit bed and what was going to happen in it.

Une was no different.

Such joys made her faintly freckled face beautifully glow. And yet there was still something that she couldn't get out of her head. This pleasing, joyful moment could never be repeated. This was so enjoyable only because she was never planning on doing it ever again.

"We shall dig a large hole in the mountaintop's black earth and bury our secret love in a coffin."

I think that's how Yaso Saijo's poem went, thought Une.

"A love whereof one cannot speak, thereof must be kept silent even after the grass grows over our grave."

Yuuji sighed as he ate the food on his plate, shooting Une loathsome stares between each bite. She nodded and smiled back at him. Their love was already in its coffin, halfway buried somewhere in the darkness on the summit of this mountain.

"I'd so marry you if you weren't my aunt. I wish I could, but I can't."

"Because I'm old?"

"That's part of it."

"Oh, you're gonna pay for that."

Une glared at him until Yuuji burst into mirthful laughter, unable to hold it in anymore.

A woman who wore such a kind smile did not look like someone who had just buried her love's coffin. Even Une herself believed that. But she never even spared a second thought about spending another night like this with Yuuji just to once again experience that euphoria. Une held that determination closely like a hidden dagger as she smiled, now able to look back fondly at her split personality. This was what made life such a joy for women.

The waiter pulled a bottle covered in droplets of condensation out of the wine cooler to pour her another glass.

That Was All It Would Ever Be

Maybe this is all Chiki's fault. It was supposed to go well, but things simply didn't fall into place where they were supposed to for some reason. What should I do now? Why did things turn out this way?

It's about Hori. I fell in love with him. He was a young man but only six years younger than me. I wouldn't be able to tell you why I like him even if you asked. He's just your average guy with nothing really special about him. I don't know how Hori feels about me, but he doesn't hate me, at least. We have a lot in common, get along well, and like a lot of the same things. Sometimes when we were talking about movie stars or books...

"O-oh, I...I have a soft spot for them," he'd say. He was just like me. Anyway, I never introduced Hori to my husband. I didn't want to weird Hori out or anything (or hear him say, *O-oh, you must have a soft spot for him*). It wasn't like I hated my husband, and it wasn't like I had anything to be embarrassed about, but...he lived to work. He simply lived in a different world from Hori and me. I hated the thought of him seeing my husband and saying, *Oh? Wow, Kaori. So this is the guy you chose to marry, huh?*

I want him to look at me and me alone. He doesn't need any

other useless data to clog his system. I'm not worried about what I'm going to do with Hori. I just like to think before I act.

I didn't want to do anything rash, but I wanted Hori all to myself while I kept my husband on the side. I wasn't thinking about making him my boyfriend, though. He was young, and I had no idea what he was thinking, either. Nevertheless, I still wanted him by my side.

By the way, it was Chiki's fault that Hori and I got close. Chiki is a small piglet toy—a finger puppet, to be exact. He has a gaudy pink-painted face made out of clay, small hands (also pink), and a haphazardly sewed-together shirt made from cheap fabric. I would stick my hand through the fabric and stuff my index finger into the carboard tube connected to Chiki's neck while my middle finger and thumb would each be in one of cardboard tubes that were his arms. Whenever I bent my index finger, it looked like Chiki was bowing. Whenever I moved my thumb, Chiki waved his left hand.

It's the simplest of finger puppets, mere child's play, but Chiki has the cutest little face. He has this bright-red nose, and his eyes are massively wide. He looks very cheerful. I'm afraid of having a pet (I've had plenty of cats die on me before), so I never had anything in my adult life that made me go, "Awww, so cute!"

I had a miscarriage when I was younger, and I still can't have kids now at thirty years old. Regardless, just like how I don't think my husband is cute, I never really thought that dolls or stuffed animals were that cute, either. Maybe that was why I fell in love. After all, I had never had anything cute that I wanted to dote on. I was just satisfied with my husband loving me; I thought that was enough. Parents of girls all seem to believe in the myth that women are happy as long as they're loved and shown affection, but I think women are always aimlessly groping for something they can love and be affectionate to.

I placed Chiki on my right hand and moved his head and arms.

"Do you think Hori's coming today?" I asked him.

"I dun think so. He isn't scheduled to visit, after all," Chiki replied with a shake of his head. His voice was adorably hoarse like a little boy's. Of course, I was the one doing the voice, but it really does feel like Chiki is speaking when I look at him. His face is only half the size of my palm, but he's extremely expressive, in my opinion.

"Oh… He's not coming, huh?"

"You can't call him, neither. He's out meeting other customers, which is why he's not gonna be in today. I know dat for a fact," claimed Chiki with a lisp. Chiki is a little boy in Hori's and my eyes. Not a little girl, for whatever reason…

I'd purchased Chiki at a night stall on July 25 at the Tenjin-san Flea Market during the summer festival at Osaka Tenmangu Shrine. On this day, large boats parade upstream and are met by another ritual boat. The festival is always packed, but Hori and I decided to go to Tenjin-san that day. This was the first time we ever went anywhere alone together.

I make fake flowers for a living. First, I dye fabrics and tulle, then use a type of soldering iron to shape them into flower petals. They're the flowers people use when making hats and bouquets. I make intricate, beautiful flowers as well for something known as intimation flower art, and I used to run a workshop teaching how to do it, but I now mainly work on making what are called bridal fashion flowers. These are the flowers brides use on their head-dresses, wedding dresses, and reception dresses.

I get the sketches and materials from the designer. After that, I think about where I'm going to put the roses or other small flowers on the veil or clothing based on what I was given, then get working on seeing it to fruition. I use a lot of fantastically colored flowers like gold or blue roses as well. Wedding attire has been getting flashier and more colorful every year. Some people even wear solid-white wedding dresses covered with small pastel roses; others decorate their sleeves with gold flowers.

Demand for gorgeous, colorful bridal clothing that gets everyone's attention has been escalating by the day. Wedding venues and rental dress shops have been receiving orders for newer and newer dresses to the point that they can't keep up, which is why I've been getting more work lately as well.

Nowadays, I pay a housewife, who I used to teach at my workshop, to make small flowers and leaves for me. It's my job to take those pieces and make the finished product, along with the most technical, difficult pieces of clothing, such as the veil or headpiece.

I like my job, and I get a lot of freedom to create what I want. Whenever the clothing companies or designers compliment my work, it motivates me all the more to work even harder. My husband doesn't seem to be thrilled about me dedicating myself to my job, but he doesn't seem to be against it, either. His own workday is extremely busy, and he works late every day. By the time he gets home at night, he's so exhausted and cranky. He almost never eats dinner at home.

My husband spends far more time with his coworkers than he does with me. Whenever I think he's back early for a change, he's immediately stuffing something into the trunk of his car.

"What are you doing?" I'd ask him.

"I'm going to America tomorrow on a two-week business trip."

"Oh."

"I didn't tell you?"

No, he never did.

He wasn't trying to be a jerk. He honestly believed he'd told me, but he simply forgot. Work seems to be the only thing that's ever on his mind, after all.

Sometimes, he gets calls from the office on our home phone, but he never seems bothered by it. In fact, he seems thrilled. He gets so caught up in the conversation, as if he has this sweet sense of camaraderie with his colleagues. There's even a hint of satisfaction in his cheerful voice—something sexually intoxicating that makes my heart skip a beat.

Work and friendship.

And if that isn't enough, there's a competitive streak between them that makes their friendship nicely flexible, malleable.

My husband is thirty-five years old, and he seems to be in a work environment that he absolutely loves. Plus, the camaraderie among his coworkers seems to be what gets him going in the morning—the glue that holds his life together. His satisfaction put me at ease because I could live my secret life without having to worry. He can keep himself entertained and fulfilled all on his own.

I had no idea he'd be this low-maintenance.

I resigned myself to that thought. I'd always sensed that he was dedicated his work. He never seemed to want children or anything like that, either. It was only after I started this job that I stopped being annoyed at how he was "playing without me." Ever since then, I've actually felt relieved that he's not home often, whether it be a business trip or overtime. Besides, my own work has me visiting countless department stores, fashion shows, and wedding venues.

Whenever the flowers I make are a hit, it pushes me even harder to breathe new, fresh air into my work, which is why I buy so many foreign wedding dress books. I've started going to the movies lately as well, and I even buy and make clothes for myself, since I like to dress up now. And I finally have my own money! My husband is very Americanized; he used to only give me money for daily necessities.

"I can't trust you with that much cash. You'd spend every last cent I gave you. You know what they say: 'If your head is wax, don't walk in the sun.' You'd eat through all our savings bit by bit."

I didn't think that, but I guess it might have looked like that from my husband's point of view. Nevertheless, my work pays very well, to my delight, and I haven't told my husband that, either. I've only told a few people about how much I make.

I've surprisingly been able to relate to and understand my husband more ever since my business became my hobby as well. It's not like I fell in love with him all over again, but I can now see why he enjoys himself so much, because I also love what I do for a living.

I used to be a little jealous of how close my husband was with his colleagues, but I can empathize with him now to the point where I'm like, *Yeah, I don't blame him.* Whenever he's busy with work, our cuddle time is over in the blink of an eye, and I only get a taste of love, even though this should be when we are affectionate the most. And yet now I think about those habits of his and go, *Yep... That's about right.*

I once thought that there was something lacking about a relationship whose void is filled only with understanding and empathy, although there was nothing I could have done about it. Plus, I'm a necessity to my husband. Sometimes, his coworkers (and their wives) come over to our place for dinner parties, and I make sure to pretend like my husband and I are really close, because I know that's what he wants. There are always a lot of couples who have lived abroad before, so the parties tend to be very lively. That's when I play the role of a great partner to my husband. My acting chops are more than up to snuff for him. I wear a white crepe de chine blouse with tight, trendy blue jeans and a platinum necklace with matching earrings. My hair is very short, which I know gathers the attention of both men and women alike. I pretend to be a wife who's loved by her husband and who always gets her way, and my husband pretends to be the smiling, sweet, devoted man who dotes on me. Even after the party is over and the guests go home, we're sometimes still giddy.

You have the happiest home life I've ever seen! You don't have any children, but you two seem to be so close and perfect together. Talk about a successful marriage!

That was surely the impression we left on my husband's boss and his wife when they came over, and we had plenty of evidence to back that up. Things like this were extremely beneficial to my husband at the workplace, given his position there. Our successful performances left us intoxicated even after the party had ended.

"Kaori, care for a drink?"

My husband took a bottle of leftover white wine out of the bucket of mostly melted ice.

"Sure."

That was all we needed to say to each other. After that, we hopped into the bath together and gave each other more love than usual—slower and steadier love. This wasn't love rekindled in the heat of the moment, though. It was more like, *Yes! We did it, partner!* We were celebrating this little show that we'd pulled off.

It was the same whenever we were invited to someone else's house for a party. I would wear a black, broad-brimmed hat and a dark-red velvet trench coat that had this vintage, elegant style to it like something from the good old days. I had a red grosgrain ribbon on my black hat, and when I would take my hat and coat off at the door, I would be wearing a leopard-print blouse with silk, black skinny pants. In other words, I always let my clothing do the talking for me and go with whatever my husband wants to do. Nevertheless, I like to pretend that I actually love parties and I'm truly excited about being there deep down. Before long, the act becomes a part of me, and I actually begin to genuinely enjoy myself at these parties. But by the end of it, I'd still feel like, *Great performance today, partner! Looks like the guests bought the act hook, line, and sinker!* I wasn't unhappy with my life, however, because I felt that everything was going well, and that was what mattered most.

Hori works for a bridal fashion company and comes in to pick up the products I make once or twice a week. Young men in his position normally came in, checked if the amount matched the order, and made sure that everything was just as the designer specified before promptly leaving without even really saying a word to me. Hori, however, would carefully observe the headpieces and flowers I made, saying things like:

"Wow, these are very stylish."

"Such a delicate color palette."

And before I even knew it, I was in love with him. It's hard to tell his age based on appearance alone, but he's apparently twenty-four years old and single. He's tall, on the thin side, and is average looks-wise. And he's pale, to boot. His hair is slightly brown and pin straight. His physique is nothing to write home about, either. Calling him scrawny would be a compliment, in fact. But for some reason, I fell in love with him.

"This crimson orchid looks really flashy at first glance, but there's something refined and pure about it," he told me. Here was someone who understood.

"Everyone keeps saying to make my flowers flashier, but I just can't come up with eye-popping, gaudy designs. Everything I make turns out cutesy," I replied.

"You're right, everyone wants flashy nowadays… The reception dresses people are wearing lately are starting to look like something out of Arabian Nights or those carp streamers people hang on Children's Day. They're way too loud. But I guess there has to be something about them. After all, you see people at weddings everywhere from Kushiro in the north to Kagoshima in the south wearing flashy dresses like that. What is with young people these days?

Am I right? The modern Japanese person is obsessed with flashy things. Maybe all young folks want to be celebrities?"

Hori joked as if he wasn't young himself.

I liked the genuine, mild-mannered way he smiled. I liked the reserved way he laughed, too. When I first realized I liked him, it felt like something in my heart had been triggered and there was no way to stop it from escalating. I immediately got the urge to talk to Hori about music, books, movies—just anything, and that's how it all started.

Hori didn't act like he knew something when he didn't like a lot of young people do. That's why after I first met him, I didn't think, *Wow! That was some fine acting again, Kaori!* I could be myself, smile, and laugh when I was with him. We only talked for ten, fifteen minutes whenever he visited, but I was so happy every day he was scheduled to come in. For whatever reason, there was something very comforting and familiar about him, as if we'd met somewhere before. I felt as if I'd known him in a past life.

One day, when I was making flowers, I suddenly felt like looking through a photo book called *A Hundred Years of Early Modern Japanese History*, which I grabbed off my husband's bookshelf. When I flipped through the pages about wartime, I found various pictures of the atrocities committed by the Empire of Japan's army across China. One of the pictures was of a young man—I don't know if he was a member of some guerrilla force or a spy or just an ordinary farmer, but he had his arms tied behind his back and was about to be executed by Japanese soldiers. He had pin-straight hair and clear eyes with sunken-in cheeks, just like Hori. His bright, clear eyes were calm; it looked as if he were asking the people about to execute him, *You sure you wanna do this? You sure you're really okay with this?* There was a hint of derision in his firm, heroic gaze.

But maybe I'm just overthinking things. Maybe he was frozen in fear and despair as he lay on the verge of death, and his eyes were randomly staring off into space as he kneeled in a daze. That tiny photograph burned itself into my mind, and maybe Hori's delicate frame reminded me of it. But there's no way I could tell him, *Hey, you kind of look just like this one POW who got executed*, so I've been keeping this to myself.

Having Hori around became very convenient after he got used to coming over to my house. He could handle basic repairs for electronics that my husband wouldn't even touch, or help clean up—basically whatever I needed help with when he came over on Sundays. My husband is never home on Sunday. Whenever he had any spare time, he'd be entertaining clients or meeting coworkers on the golf course, so I would invite Hori over for a little lunch.

I don't own a cat personally, but I feed a stray mother and two kittens that hang out in my backyard. When Hori came over, he gently reached out, and they let him pet their heads while they calmly ate. There's also a weasel that took up residence in my backyard, but when it was passing through my garden that day, it suddenly noticed Hori and froze in place with its eyes locked on him for some time.

"I love animals. I want to get a pet and live in the countryside one day," Hori said, and I immediately agreed with him. Hanging out with cats and dogs in my bare feet, riding horses—that would be the life, but it was a life that would never happen. I would continue my act with my husband while thinking, *My acting was flawless today!* and Hori would travel from Kushiro to Kagoshima, selling bridal fashion all along the way.

"A city mouse like me wouldn't be able to handle it, though," he joked. I could easily tell he was born in Osaka. He was very nonchalant about everything and highly adaptable.

One night, we went to Tenjin-san together. There were so many people crowding the bridge that we couldn't see the ritual boat procession, so we decided to go to the main shrine to worship and bought a finger puppet at one of the stalls outside. The festival music in the background was very Osaka-ish, really lively and busy: *dum-dum-tss-chiki, dum-tss-chiki, dum-dum-tss-chiki, dum-tss-chiki.*

The music at Kyoto's Gion Festival is slower and more drawn out like: *dummm-tsss-chiiiki.* People in Osaka always complain that it bores them to death, but the music nonetheless got stuck in my head, which was why I named my new finger puppet piglet Chiki.

We went out for pasta in southern Osaka after that. It was the first time I'd ever wandered the streets of Osaka at night with a younger man. The restaurant was a tiny hole-in-the-wall, but it felt so alive. We drank wine and had so much fun with Chiki as well. Hori's pale complexion and soft skin became slightly flushed.

Even though I couldn't do any impressive tricks like ventriloquism, I placed Chiki on my right hand and said: "Hey, I'm Chiki," in an extremely believable child's voice. "Quick question. Are you two just friends or…?"

"'Or'…? What do you think?" I teased him, but Chiki shook his head and asked more directly:

"Are you guys dating? Or not?"

"This fella's a little too forward, and annoyingly immature," Hori said.

"He's still got to learn his manners, huh?" I replied. Chiki then pointed right at my face.

"Don'cha gotta hurry home tonight?"

There was something hilarious about how Chiki said "don'cha" whenever he was trying to lecture me.

"Don'cha think your husband'll start to worry?"

"That's nothing a child like you has to be concerned about."

"But he's gonna be real mad if you come home late."

"It's fine. He's working late tonight, too," I replied.

"Huh. You both always go home late?"

"Yep."

"Why d'you live together, then?"

To keep up the act. For appearances. But would Chiki even understand that?

"What d'you like to do for fun?" Chiki asked me.

"Good question... I guess I like to drink wine and daydream, kind of like what I'm doing now. And I like being with you, Chiki."

"D'you like bein' with Hori?"

"He's really fun to be around."

"You like him?"

"Oh, well...I—"

"Chiki, quit it. Stop teasing the adults." Hori smacked Chiki's peach-colored head in a fluster.

"Owie. Why'd you hit me?"

"Because you don't know when to keep your mouth shut."

"Dun pretend you weren't curious."

"Shh! Chiki, come on. Stop."

"Why? You like Kaori, don'cha?"

"Sorry about him," I said. "He's being such a brat."

We happened to go out for a drink after that as well. I placed Chiki in my bag at the bar, and while we were drinking...

"Havin' a *third* drink? Don'cha know you're not gonna be able to go home if you have that much?!" I made Chiki shout at Hori.

"So what if we can't go home tonight? We're adults. Mind your own business."

"Ooh, are you two gonna be naughty? Is that what's gonna happen?"

It was all so absurd that I burst into laughter. Hori and I probably used jokes to gradually help us relax because like they say, "if your head is wax, don't walk in the sun." With Chiki around, we could simply laugh off how naughty we were being.

Chiki turned his gaze at Hori to protest, but Hori immediately covered Chiki's mouth.

"Keep quiet, you stupid little oinker…"

"Takes one to know one. Owie, you're gonna make me even stupider!"

Their exchange was so ridiculous that I clutched my stomach and cackled. Hori's a real joker, to my surprise, for someone who looks like a POW about to be executed. The more of his sense of humor he shows me, the more fun I have. He comes off as a really mild-mannered man, but deep down, he's kind of like a treasure chest filled with all sorts of fun stuff.

That day, Chiki became the center of our universe.

"How's Chiki?" Hori asked whenever he called me.

I keep Chiki in one corner of my workroom, stuck on top of an old bottle of lotion wrapped with a towel. Otherwise, Chiki would be lying face flat on my table like a broken marionette while scraps of fabric and dust gradually covered his body.

At first glance, Chiki looked like a complete doofus with his goofy nose and slack-jawed mouth, but I learned that there was much more to him than that.

"Your husband'll still be on his business trip dis Sunday, right?"

"Oh, hmm… Good question."

"You wanna go for a drive, don'cha? Hee-hee-hee, can't wait."

Oh, you little…

"You're way too smart for your age," I said before smacking Chiki.

But it turned out just like Chiki said it would. We went up to Hokusetsu in the mountains that Sunday. My husband had left the car behind, so Hori ended up driving. I held Chiki in my left hand and showed him the view from the window. It was still hot, since autumn had just started, but the wind smelled differently already.

"Ah, da wind feels sooo good," Chiki blissfully commented. While it was really me talking, Chiki's voice was always so adorable, just like a child's.

"The wind does feel nice, doesn't it?"

"I'm hungry… Hurry up and feed me," Chiki whined.

"Who brought the brat? Because I don't remember us inviting any brats with us." Hori played along, which made it all the more hilarious.

The forest greenery had become a bit more subdued, and even the abundant weeds were losing steam. What stood out the most, however, was how different the clouds were now: so fluffy and light.

There were some willows along the riverside and a nice shaded area as well. It was still a little early, but if we kept going straight, we would suddenly end up in the middle of a massive apartment complex.

"Let's eat here."

So we ended up having a picnic by the riverside. After covering the table with an old tablecloth, Hori and I brought our lunches over. The perfectly square *shunkei*-lacquered lunch boxes were stuffed with a variety of food.

"W-wow… Now, this makes me happy." Hori started smacking his lips.

He was once again keeping Chiki occupied while I was getting out the cups and chopsticks.

"Chiki, you've never had such a wonderful feast out in nature like this before, have you?"

"I've had a tough life…"

Now that he mentioned it, this would be my first picnic, too, although my husband often had picnics at the golf course with his work buddies. I used to watch him entertain himself without me and started wondering if I'd slowly wasted my life away like someone with a wax head walking into the sun.

Inside the lunch boxes were meatballs, chicken meatloaf, braised vegetables with salad, dried plums, and burdock root—all of which Hori seemed to love. Contrary to his delicate frame and pale complexion, he seemed to be in very good health and had a healthy appetite to go with it. I'd never seen someone eat my cooking with such enthusiasm before.

He's so young, I thought fondly. Hori had told me that the food at his boarding house was awful, which probably explained why he ate until his stomach was on the verge of exploding.

"You're such a pig!" I made Chiki shout. "Got anythin' else you wanna say, Hori?"

"No, I think I'm good."

"Betcha wish you could eat like dis every day."

"You know it."

Hori wore a dazed, innocent expression as he sprawled out over the picnic blanket with his arms crossed behind his head. It was a very quiet day, with only a few cars driving down the prefectural road in the distance every once in a while.

"Chiki, go find me a wife, will ya?"

"Wives don't grow on trees, y'know. Find one for yourself."

"Oh, shut up."

I ate a lot as well, so I was feeling great. I usually ate alone, so most of the time, I couldn't even remember what I ate even right after I finished it. Plus, there was something really nice about relaxing outside in the fresh air with a full stomach.

"Those eggs with soybeans in them were amazing. Soybean omelets, I think is what they're called," Hori said to Chiki. "I've had chive omelets before, but omelets with rice and black sesame? Incredible. Plus, Chiki, there's something aesthetically pleasing when you wrap it all up in dried seaweed."

"I liked da chicken meatloaf. Da burdock root was real good, too. Anyway, no more food talk. You got any plans after dis?"

"Hmm… What do you think I should do, Chiki?"

Hori was very calm, which reminded me of that POW's clear eyes moments before he was executed. Maybe Hori was more daring than I thought.

"You're only gonna make things worse if you go *too* far, Hori," Chiki retorted.

I thought about all kinds of situations and places we could go. There was one place I wouldn't mind going, since I had feelings for him, but that'd just create problems for me, so I had to really focus on making sure things didn't get complicated.

"You're right. I wouldn't want to take her anywhere that'd complicate things for her too much."

Was Hori trying to sound me out? Heh-heh.

But I was interested.

"You oughtta pack it up and get outta here while you still can!"

"Oh, shut up," I joked while smacking Chiki on the head.

"Hori's gonna wanna take you to places if you stay here too long, don'cha know?" Chiki shouted.

I couldn't help but laugh. This was exactly what I liked about Hori. He was so funny. But if I just made someone like that my lover, then that was all it would ever be. I took Chiki out of Hori's hand.

"Yeah, Hori. This is about more than just getting laid!" I made Chiki yell.

Hori smacked Chiki's head, gazed at the vast blue sky, then slowly lay back down on the ground. It looked like he was going to take a nap.

Already Finished Packing

Hideo had been very quiet since morning, as if he were in a bad mood, but Eriko pretended not to notice and continued acting normal. Nevertheless, she'd been racking her brain all day to find out why he was in a foul mood, but she couldn't come up with a single reason.

I can't imagine what's wrong.

They had watched TV together last night and were sound asleep by eleven, so there was no reason for Hideo to be upset, and yet here he was—sulking. There was something miserable about seeing a massive, bulky man in a foul mood. He was around a hundred and eighty centimeters tall with a hefty amount of meat on him, and despite being forty-four years old, he had a somewhat childlike face. Eriko, who was forty-two, looked younger than her age due to her small frame, so they were sometimes mistaken for a couple in their thirties thanks to Hideo's boyish face.

But whenever he was in a bad mood, he looked like a child having a fit. Hideo drank his coffee and ate his breakfast of buttered toast and bacon in silence, then began getting changed.

"I'm gonna stop by Tennoji today," he murmured while tying his tie.

Seriously? thought Eriko as she calmly replied, "I guess I won't make dinner tonight, then, if you're going to be late."

"I don't know when I'll get back."

"I'm going to go out to eat, then."

"I might be home for dinner."

"All we've got is *ochazuke*."

"I don't care what we have for dinner!"

What's he in such a huff about? Eriko thought he was being ridiculous.

Hideo's mother, his ex-wife, Kyoko, and their three children lived in Tennoji in southern Osaka. He would visit them on occasion, although not with any regularity. And every time he was going to Tennoji, he would be in a bad mood.

To tell the truth, Hideo's current wife, Eriko, wasn't thrilled about him going to Tennoji to spend time with his ex and their kids like a big happy family, so it wouldn't be unnatural if she got angry. And yet it was Hideo who was in a foul mood. He seemed to be acting this way because he was anticipating his wife being in a bad mood. Perhaps he was afraid of Eriko getting upset with him, so he used this anger as a suit of armor to protect himself. He also seemed to be annoyed at his own ineptness, since he was unable to get around offending Eriko.

"Takeshi got in trouble at school," Hideo grumbled.

"Oh."

Takeshi was Hideo's second-oldest son and currently in high school.

"Apparently, he punched one of his teachers."

"He's at that age, huh…?" Eriko muttered, although she absolutely did not care one bit. She just wished he would handle those problems when he was in Tennoji instead of bringing them home with him. He may have been their father, but he didn't live with them.

"Is that really all you have to say?"

Eriko didn't respond. Hideo was extremely irritated, and really, was there anything further she could say? She couldn't exactly criticize him at the moment.

"It's going to be cold tonight," Eriko stated, changing the subject. "You should make sure to dress warm before you go."

"..."

Hideo was usually a very good-humored individual, which made it hard to really tell what kind of mood he was in. But he was always in a foul mood whenever he went to Tennoji. Perhaps he wanted to show Eriko that he wasn't going because he liked to, so he made it seem like it was a chore. Regardless, being in a bad mood was the worst thing he could do.

When a man and a woman live together, being in a bad mood is like only having one chair was what Eriko wanted to tell him. *It's a game of musical chairs where all the person sitting has to do is not stand up to win. The other person isn't allowed to sit.*

They couldn't both be in a bad mood. The only time a couple living together should be in a bad mood is when they break up. If two people still want to live together, they need to understand that there is always one chair and one chair only. Of course, Hideo was rarely in a bad mood, and he never behaved high-handedly, either.

Eriko always thought he had eyes like a basset hound, but never once did she say it. He looked so pathetic and weak when he looked up with his droopy, wide-set eyes, which were extremely brazen whenever he was flattered and spoiled. Eriko kind of liked that duality about him. She even found it cute from time to time.

She didn't like it when he was in a bad mood, though.

Eriko and Hideo had been married for ten years. It was his second marriage and her first. Eriko had been working and single until she was thirty-two years old, so she had absolutely no plans to get married unless it was going to be really fun. She was creating a PR magazine with a Hanshinkan sake company, and she had been working at her current job for a long time. She enjoyed it; she had a lot of influence and knew a lot of people. Eriko had gotten used to life in Osaka, an easy place to live as long as you didn't pursue your own ideals. She met Hideo, who was thirty-three at the time and had been married to his then-wife for around seven or eight years, at work. The first time they went drinking together...

"I'm thinking about getting a divorce."

Hideo had brought up a problem he was having that night. He didn't get a divorce because of Eriko. He had fallen out of love with his then-wife a long time ago but stayed with her because of their complicated family circumstances.

Hideo wasn't his parents' biological son. He was adopted and succeeded the family's Tennoji estate, which then took in Kyoko. They were a married couple adopted into the family in the locals' eyes, essentially. In the midst of discussing breaking things off, they ended up having three kids. After Hideo's father died, they ended up getting divorced, and Kyoko found a new place to live. She left the kids behind as well. Hideo was raising the children with his mother for a while, but within a year, Kyoko got remarried. He seemed refreshed and cheerful after that.

"Want to get married? I want to get back the life I missed out on. I wanna boogie. Now. Have some fun," he told Eriko.

Hearing him say he wanted to "boogie" was so funny to Eriko that she took a liking to him. But his kids were a problem. Eriko also worked, so their only two options were to work and send money for the kids or adopt them.

"I can't take care of any kids, so I'll pay child support," she told him up front.

This was a crucial moment. She was being calm and reasonable with her decision and thought she shouldn't say anything she didn't really mean just to look good. Fortunately, his mother in Tennoji was still in very good health and agreed to raise the children, so Hideo moved into an apartment with Eriko in Toyonaka.

Eriko stayed at the same job she always had, but every month, a lot of her money ended up going to Hideo's family in Tennoji. As a result, even though were both working, they didn't have any savings. Nevertheless, she was glad she got married. It wasn't only Hideo. Eriko also enjoyed the life she missed out on.

She never went to Tennoji herself, but sometimes, she and Hideo would bring his kids, who were in elementary school at the time, to the zoo in Tennoji or Hanshin Park, where she enjoyed being mom for a day. Her name was on Hideo's family register, but she wasn't listed as the kids' adoptive mother, and they always called her their aunt from Toyonaka. The two eldest were boys, and the youngest was a girl. Hideo's daughter had her hair cut in a bob and wore shorts just like his two sons. Eriko wasn't around children often, so she enjoyed talking to them and spending time with them. One time, Hideo ended up bringing the two boys to Toyonaka with him.

Their house in Tennoji was old and run-down—in other words, it was a very spacious house with many rooms, but it was dark. Hideo's boys seemed to be amazed by how small yet bright his and Eriko's modern apartment was. They ran around the apartment, opening each and every door and making a huge mess. That was why Hideo decided to give them a bath. Once he got out of the tub, he put in his boys, who started splashing with joy and giggling. They were apparently starving for attention from their father, and when it was time for them to go back home to Tennoji, the younger son was on the verge of tears.

"Why don't you let them stay the night?" suggested Eriko.

The boys' faces briefly lit up with joy.

"No," Hideo flatly replied. "Go home. You know what train to take." Then he added, "Oh, and make sure you don't lose the money I gave you."

"Why don't you walk them to the station?" Eriko asked instinctively.

"They're boys. They can find their way home on their own."

The children began putting on their shoes in resignation, then walked out the door and said good-bye. Whether they were saying it to their father or Eriko was a mystery.

When they were frantically squealing with joy in the bathtub, Eriko noticed the metallic taste of jealousy at the back of her throat, but she still felt bad for them when they gave up and left. She was overcome with the feeling that she'd stolen their father from them. Hideo, on the other hand, seemed to be in a good mood.

"You gotta give them opportunities to be independent from time to time," he said. It sounded like he was trying to keep his life with Eriko separate.

A year had gone by when one morning, Hideo mentioned, "I'm going to Tennoji. A carpenter's coming over today…"

"Oh. Fixing the place up?"

The house in Tennoji was old, so Hideo usually had to do any repairs when something broke, which he always did a good job at. But seeing as they hired a professional, perhaps it was something more complicated than usual.

"The annex needs a lot of work."

"Are you going to have it rebuilt?"

"Yeah." Hideo was in a bad mood. "She's back."

"Who's back?"

"Who do you think?!" Hideo shouted, clearly irritated.

Yelling at me isn't going to fix anything, Eriko thought as she rolled her eyes. "Don't tell me you're talking about Kyoko."

"I am."

Kyoko's second marriage had fallen apart, and she had nowhere to go, so she returned to Tennoji and moved in with Hideo's mother. His mother was getting a little too old and tired to raise the children, so of course, she welcomed Kyoko with open arms.

Both of Kyoko's marriages had ended in failure. Maybe she was just a victim of fate, but it was hard not to see her as someone who was impulsive and never thought things through.

"Why do you want to get a divorce?" Eriko had asked Hideo that day years ago.

"She's a lazy cow. She's dense and stubborn, and once she's made up her mind, she won't move whether you push her or pull her. She's always nagging and splitting hairs over the most ridiculous things, and then she's weirdly laid-back about random stuff and loves to 'fool around,'" Hideo answered, disheartened.

Eriko had never met Kyoko, but she'd heard rumors about her from her cousin once. Apparently, Kyoko was an irresponsible slob. She didn't use clothespins when hanging out laundry to dry, so the wet clothes would get blown away by the wind. She would also forget to go pick them up until later that night or even the next morning from time to time. Sometimes, when she ran out of clean clothes, she went shopping for new ones instead of washing the dirty ones. She constantly forgot to pay the phone or electric bill, and whenever you opened the refrigerator, there would be something in it that had already gone bad.

Eriko and Hideo never talked about Kyoko ever since they got married, but Eriko always had this vague image of her in the back of her mind—this "lazy cow," as Hideo had described.

"When did this all happen?"

"Half a year ago."

"Oh. I had no idea," Eriko said. She became strangely annoyed. If Kyoko had moved back to Tennoji half a year ago, then surely, Hideo would have seen her at least three or four times, since that was how many times he had gone back these past six months to see his mother and children.

"So Kyoko moved back in six months ago? Why didn't you tell me?"

"Because I didn't want to upset you."

While it wasn't a pleasant thing to find out, Eriko always imagined that her husband was living another life with just his kids while she wasn't around. Never did she imagine that the ex-wife was back in the picture. Eriko had seen Hideo with his children countless times; it was a part of her life. She had seen him bathe with his boys as they squealed with glee; she'd witnessed his young daughter seated comfortably in his lap, his arms around her. Eriko imagined it was like that whenever he went back to Tennoji. But adding his ex-wife, Kyoko, to the equation made it impossible for her to envision what kind of life he was living. And the fact that he kept this to himself for half a year made it all the more shocking.

"Why not tell me? You could've just said that Kyoko got a divorce and was back."

"What would that have solved?"

"Your mother didn't tell me anything, either."

"Why would she? It has nothing to do with you."

He may have been right, but Eriko could no longer tell him to "enjoy himself and have dinner with his family" now that she knew Kyoko was there. Nevertheless, that hang-up slowly faded over the years. After spending so many years with Hideo, his life with her probably started to slightly outweigh his old life—time-wise, at the very least. That was how Eriko started to feel. The only time she thought about Tennoji was when she sent money to the house there every month. After a while, Hideo's mother had to be hospitalized, and his oldest son started college, so they ended up needing even more money.

Kyoko didn't work, but she was apparently doing chores around the house.

Why do I have to work my ass off to take care of someone else's family? Eriko thought from time to time, but when she thought of the payment as if she were paying for her time with Hideo, she figured, *I guess this isn't all that expensive.*

The children stopped clinging to Hideo so much, perhaps because having their mother around pacified them or because they were simply at that age where they wanted their distance. As a result, they basically stopped coming to Toyonaka. People were gradually able to live grander lifestyles the past few years, so Eriko and Hideo started going on small vacations as well. While it was in a slightly inconvenient location in the suburbs, they moved to an apartment in the mountains in Nishinomiya. They got the place in Eriko's name, since the house in Tennoji was under Hideo's name, which he always had on his mind. Whenever the roof was leaking or a shutter broke, Hideo would pay for it as if he ran two households.

Nevertheless, Eriko found her life with Hideo great. They got to "boogie" together in her mind. Hideo worked hard and a lot, which was hard to believe if he were judged only by his massive body, and he always cleaned the bath, wiped the glass doors, and took on various other chores without ever complaining. He was also the one who would come home and immediately try to make whatever unusual, tasty side dish he found when he was out drinking with Eriko.

"I thought about it all night until I figured it out this morning. That dressing had peanut butter in it," he would say. He was a big man, which meant he had a big appetite and loved delicious food (his favorite being Eriko's home cooking). With that being said, Eriko wasn't especially good at cooking. Their taste buds and preferences simply started to match each other's after living together for so long.

"I'm so glad I married you, Eriko! I finally know how fun life can be thanks to you."

It wasn't long before Hideo felt this way.

Eriko had a very busy job, so she would often come home late a few times every month. She had an established PR magazine now that was published bimonthly, but with success came more responsibility. She began taking the chair at small meetings, was left in charge of handling interviews and photography, and was given a seemingly endless supply of work. Eriko wasn't full of ambition or anything like that, but she was secretly developing her talents to keep the position she was in.

Even though she wasn't technically an editor, her work helped her learn the importance of connections and meeting new people. She had to meet many people and had to have them like her as well. Eriko was skinny and petite with a fair complexion. She had a dimple in her right cheek whenever she laughed and sparkling, white teeth that were perfectly straight. She kept her hair casual and short, along with her attire: jeans and a sweater, which made her always look like she had just gotten out of college. She was even told, "I've known you for quite a while now, but I still can't tell how old you are. I mean, I've known you ever since the chairman was still alive," by one of the big shots when she was at the Chamber of Commerce and Industry.

"I just turned thirty," Eriko said, smiling. She had actually turned forty-two that year.

She enjoyed her life of picking up that leftover work that needed to be done in her little corner of Osaka. She felt fulfilled. For years, she watched the ginkgo leaves in Midosuji turn gold, then blue, then gold once more before they fell to the ground. Whenever a new big shot took over for the old one at a company, she would go straight to the new CEO for an interview, smile, and say she heard they were drinking buddies with a CEO from company XYZ while trying to create a bond. The old Eriko would never have been able to do this. It was far too frightening. In the past, when she finally got to meet the chairman of the Chamber of Commerce and Industry, she immediately broke down in tears when he simply looked at her and asked, "What is it you want to know?"

While people always said they couldn't tell how old Eriko was, they had an even harder time guessing whether she had a husband. There was no one outside of her work life who knew, but she had Hideo, so she felt excited to work. Whenever Eriko was late coming home from work, Hideo would always make something simple for dinner and wait for her.

"You didn't have to wait for me to eat."

"Eating without you would be so lonely. I enjoy dinner because I'm with you. Besides, food is tasteless without you. It's like eating sand."

Those words were enough to make Eriko stop caring about the monthly expenses she was suffering due to his second family.

I guess this isn't all that expensive was how she felt when she thought about her life with Hideo, no matter how much it cost her. Of course, Eriko would never tell Hideo that, though. She would, however, show him her little dimple as she flashed her small, pearly white teeth. Eriko, as petite as she was, had both small hands and small feet, and she looked even smaller when she stood next to the massive man that Hideo was. Eriko was apparently the cutest little delicate doll in the entire world to Hideo.

Eriko had decided that she didn't want kids. She went back and forth on the idea a little when they first got married, but she felt that they had already built a comfortable foundation for their lives and that there was no room for any children. She would rather be spoiled herself. That was what she thought, so that was probably why she got jealous when she heard Hideo's children squealing with joy when they came over and were having a good time.

Nevertheless, Eriko enjoyed her quiet life with Hideo while his kids got older. But the more fun she was having, the more uneasy she started to feel. She didn't know why, though. After Hideo went to work, Eriko would clean up before leaving the house herself. Since they were near the mountains, the temperature was slightly colder than the average flat city. Curtains would even freeze to the window during the winter if they weren't careful. Eriko rode her bike to the station through the fresh, cold air. But when she got on the rocking train heading to the city, she realized why she was anxious—or discontent, to be exact.

While Hideo probably didn't mean for it to be this way, it started to feel like his home in Tennoji was his real home and his home with her was his secondary residence. Eriko was legally his wife, and she had been married and living with him for the past ten years, but she didn't know how Hideo viewed and mentally allocated his life. After all, his kids, ex-wife, and elderly adoptive mother were all in Tennoji, where he had a house and land in his name.

Even the son who was causing trouble at school, which in return was causing trouble for their family, had a strong presence in Eriko's household. He used to take baths from time to time with his father and squeal with joy, but now he was throwing fists at school, which Eriko believed he may have been doing because he wanted Hideo's attention. Hideo never once stayed overnight at the house in Tennoji, and that didn't start when Kyoko moved back in. He had never stayed overnight there. Nevertheless, Eriko for some reason suddenly started wondering, *Does he consider his home with me to be his second home?*

Hideo was a large man, so Eriko could curl up and fit perfectly in his arms (just like how his daughter used to curl up and fit perfectly in his lap). On cold winter nights, she could still keep warm in his embrace, even if she wasn't wearing anything, as his body wrapped around her like a blanket. It was like a vast, endless blanket that was warm and strong while not heavy. Hideo's body was like a warm, comforting imaginary blanket that would sometimes suddenly swipe her up like a passionate flying squirrel and steal her away. Eriko never got tired of being scooped up off her feet, but that passion and change of pace was special because it didn't happen every day, she felt.

Eriko felt fulfilled every moment she spent with Hideo. She was proud to be with him and happy as well, but there was something about the marriage that didn't feel real deep down inside.

She even liked his cute basset hound-like eyes when he was in a bad mood. She wondered what it meant to still feel this way about her husband even after ten years of marriage. That was just how friendly Hideo was and a testament to how well they got along, but perhaps what was making him this way was what he was experiencing at the house in Tennoji. There was actually nothing about his life with Eriko that put him in a bad mood, and he would always return to their apartment with glee.

The only time he would be in a bad mood was when he had to go to Tennoji. It was like he felt he was held back by the shackles of convention every time he reluctantly went... It was one's duty to take care of their home. Eriko worried about the whole second-house dilemma the entire day while she was at work. She finished up earlier than usual that night, but she took her time leaving the office, since Hideo wasn't going to be there when she got home. That was when he suddenly gave her a call.

"I'm going to be late tonight," he told her before briefly pausing. *"Takeshi hasn't come home yet, and nobody's seen him since this morning. He didn't go to school, either. And he knew I was coming tonight..."*

"You don't know where he went?"

"Not a clue. It's hard to believe he would run away from home..."

"Do you really think he would ever do such a thing?"

"I doubt it, but he can be a real doofus sometimes, so who knows?" Hideo seemed to be on edge. *"I'm going to wait here until he comes home tonight."*

Eriko didn't know how to respond. She didn't care whether Takeshi ran away from home or even vanished into thin air, so she couldn't work up enough energy to even attempt comforting him, no matter how unenthusiastic it would sound.

"Okay," she simply replied.

A young cameraman who she was planning on going out to eat with called her while he was still in the field and told her he was just going to go straight home. The building, which was located on the south side of Yodoyabashi Bridge, was old and run-down, but the view from the window was wonderful. The lights from the north buildings lit up the dark night, and the sky was a clear purple-blue. There wasn't much better than going for a walk toward the north side in the river breeze, taking in the view from Yodoyabashi Bridge to Oebashi Bridge, during cold winter nights such as this. Hideo's office was in Honmachi, so he would sometimes come all the way down to this building to invite her for a walk.

"Shall we?" he would say.

"Okay."

And just like that, they would walk all the way to Umeda. This didn't only happen when they first got married. They still went on long walks like this now as well. Kitashinchi in the north was expensive, so they would usually eat somewhere like Sonezaki before going home. It was basically a tradition for them to go out for cheap puffer fish hot pot on cold nights like this. Right as Eriko was about to leave the office, she got another phone call. It was Hideo again.

"Still at the office?"

"I was about to leave."

"Oh. Well, Takeshi came home."

" . . . "

"The teacher he hit is here, too, but Takeshi won't apologize."

" . . . "

"The principal's also here. Can you believe it? Anyway...I'm just glad he came back. I know worrying wasn't going to help anything, but I couldn't help it."

"…Okay."

"Where are you going?"

"To the puffer fish restaurant," she promptly replied without a second thought.

"Do they even serve single customers?"

"Yes. Puffer fish."

This seemed to strike Hideo as very sudden.

"Well, look at you. And here I am, about to go to war."

"Why don't you come with me, then? Let the teachers handle the mess."

"I can't," he replied, annoyed. *"Bye."*

He hung up. The spite in Hideo's voice when he said "Well, look at you" annoyed Eriko a little.

It's not my fault.

In reality, Eriko would never let a bratty teenager even get close to her, so she couldn't even imagine the situation. She couldn't understand why this high school kid was being so stubborn and not apologizing, and she couldn't understand why the teachers were making such a big deal out of this, either. And she was repelled by Hideo's aggravation at the emergency. Eriko took the subway to the puffer fish restaurant. She said someone would be coming to meet up with her later, then took her gloves and hat off at the table in the corner of the restaurant. After taking off her shoes, sitting down, and closing the screen door, her face immediately looked like the face of a relieved forty-two-year-old, without a dimple in sight.

The puffer fish sashimi always came on a celadon plate like petals on a cherry blossom. Eriko and Hideo always enjoyed the work of art on the plate to the point that they didn't want to eat any of it. "Be my guest," they would usually say to each other with a smile before eventually surrendering and digging in. Hideo couldn't hold his liquor, so he would only drink his single glass of hot sake, and that would be it for him. Eriko, however, would always have two glasses.

She ordered enough for two, half expecting Hideo to come, and when the food arrived, it was just like it always was. The blood comfortably rushed through her body as the hot sake made her do an emotional one-eighty. Eriko looked at her pocketbook while calling the house in Tennoji. She had never called even once before in the ten years she had been married.

"Hello?" It was a middle-aged woman's voice.

"Is Hideo there?"

"Huh? Hideo? He just got into a fight with his son, and things got physical until his oldest stepped in. They ended up breaking the glass door to the garden. Anyway, he's busy right now, so he can't come to the phone."

It was without a doubt his ex-wife, Kyoko, and for some reason, she knew it was Eriko on the other end of the line.

"Please try calling back again later," she quickly added before hanging up.

She seemed to be on edge. Eriko's first impression of her was that she seemed to be a woman who talked a lot. She didn't seem to be a lazy, slow cow at all. If anything, she seemed to be very energetic. Her first impression was shocking, but it was a world Eriko couldn't even imagine, so she felt daunted. Hideo's spiteful "Well, look at you" made a lot more sense now, since it was a world unimaginable by someone who walked across cold bridges at night with their arms around their partner before being captivated by the beauty of a plate of puffer fish.

Eriko was hurt. She felt like she was stuck in a "Well, look at you" and "He's busy right now" sandwich of parting shots. It didn't help that she felt like a mistress calling the man she was sleeping with's wife. She felt that perhaps life over there, as chaotic as it was right now, was how life was supposed to be. She was depressed that perhaps her sweet little life was nothing more than the surface of Hideo's full, rich life.

Maybe it was a woman's greed. Maybe it was jealousy. Whichever the case, Eriko wanted every single part of Hideo to herself. All of a sudden, she realized that Hideo hadn't sounded like he was in a bad mood when they last talked. Perhaps he was in a world that didn't allow him the luxury of being in a bad mood. And when Eriko thought of it like that, she felt bad for him. Nevertheless, she still didn't want to carry that baggage he had back in Tennoji together with him. After all, she did tell him that she couldn't take care of any children when they first got married. She was the one who decided to take the sweet, comfortable life in the second home. Hideo said he wanted to "boogie" and have fun, but he was slowly having to spend his life with both Eriko and his family in Tennoji.

Eriko wanted to answer the phone out of breath and panicking like Kyoko. Of course, she wanted to share the happy, sweet moments with Hideo, but she also wanted to share the hardships with him as well—moments where she could shout *He's busy now* at other women on the phone. She was starting to not know what exactly she wanted anymore. On one hand, the way Kyoko spoke made it sound like she envied how calm and uncaring Eriko could be, but on the other hand, she was probably sharing a moment and bonding with Hideo over that disastrous event. Eriko was going back and forth. She had already finished packing, but she didn't know where to go… Perhaps Kyoko, on the phone, was feeling the same way, and Eriko felt that what she packed was divided into two halves.

The water in the hot pot was boiling. Eriko picked up her chopsticks.

Taken Prisoner

Even though his lunch box was packed, Minoru still wasn't out the door.

"It's already eleven, you know," said Rie.

"I *know*!" Minoru replied sullenly. The TV was on, but his pensive gaze was only fixed idly on the screen.

He's still having second thoughts. Rie smirked.

Minoru was a very indecisive person, so it was easy to sense when he was being hesitant. His indecisiveness even annoyed himself, which ended up making him depressed, and then he'd take his anger out on Rie. But he couldn't get mad at her, because it was his fault and his fault alone that things came to this.

"You need to pour the hot water in the cup like this," she instructed calmly. She wasn't trying to sound calm; that's just how her voice naturally sounded. "Then it'll turn into miso soup. The miso and vegetables are already in the cup, so all it needs is hot water."

"..."

"You should probably start heading out if you want to arrive before it gets dark."

Rie was leisurely sipping on some coffee at the kitchen table. A tall woman, she had big hands to go with her size. Her bony hands even made the Ginori mug look small when she held it. Both Rie and Minoru loved the Italian Ginori cups and saucers with the fruit designs on them. A simple cup and saucer with a violet fruit or blue flower on them cost around thirteen thousand yen. They had been collecting these sets for years and years until they at last reached four sets, and that was around when they started going through a divorce.

"Don't think too much about it while you're driving. You'll get into an accident," Rie said with a faint smirk. "Can't have the groom getting hurt, after all."

"Ha-ha. Very funny." Minoru walked over and took a seat in the empty chair. "Pour me a cup of coffee, too, will ya?"

"Oh? Very forward, demanding a stranger make you a coffee."

"Oof. Come on. Be a good stranger and please make me some coffee."

"This is the last coffee you're ever getting from me."

"Come on, stop picking on me already."

"If you want me to stop picking on you, how about you hurry up and leave?"

"Hmm... I don't know. I feel funny. I still can't imagine never coming back here. The fact that we're gonna not be a family anymore still feels weird. It's still like, 'Am I really getting a divorce?'"

"Isn't it a little late to be saying that?"

"It feels like a dream."

"In that it makes you happy?"

"Mm, it's not that simple. It's something more complicated than being happy or sad. I still don't feel like I have the courage to split up with you."

"Well, you did."

"It hurts hearing you say that."

Minoru was three years younger than Rie. He was a large, healthy, slightly chubby man whose stomach had just started to protrude. His eyes were slightly drooping, and he had a boyish, cherubic face for a thirty-two-year-old. Minoru was also a very kindhearted man and rather popular with the ladies, but Rie found his kindness to be elusive. It was the kindness of a child: innocently cruel and full of lies.

I'd like a refund for this defective adult male, she used to think, although she nonetheless found his innocent kindness and childish ego cute. But whenever something happened, she would go right back to thinking he was defective.

He's easily swayed and indecisive, Rie thought.

Minoru had said, "It hurts hearing you say that," but she wondered if he really was pained deep down inside about going his separate way. Rie slowly filled the Ginori cup to the brim with freshly brewed coffee while Minoru watched, seemingly captivated by the cup.

"Is that your share?" he asked.

"Yep."

"Did I pack my share?"

"You did, in your bag. Two whole sets," Rie replied.

They split the cups and saucers half-and-half. Was Minoru planning on using his share, which was filled with memories of Rie and him collecting them together, with that other woman? Minoru was insensitive and indifferent, so he would probably use them with his new woman without giving it a second thought.

"You're gonna be bringing the English chair with you, right?"

He was referring an old wooden chair that they'd bought at a Western antique shop together.

"You took the hexagon clock, too, right?"

"Yeah, but, like...you told me I could take whatever I wanted, right?"

"That's fine. I was just thinking about how you're mainly taking the things we bought together..."

"Sorry. If you want it, I'll give it back. I'm just used to having the chair and the clock around. They're easy to use."

You were used to having me around more than anything, seeing as we were married for eight years, and look what happened there, Rie thought with a smirk.

"Oh yeah." Minoru placed his cup down. "Can I bring the pictures from the photo album with me, too?"

"What are you going to use those for?"

"What do you mean? If we're gonna split up, we should probably separate the pictures, too, right?"

"How considerate of you."

Minoru opened the album and carefully peeled off any photo where he was the only one in it. He didn't touch any pictures with both him and Rie in them. He apparently only wanted to bring his history and his history alone with him to the next stage in his life.

"Just take the whole album with you," recommended Rie in a particularly insouciant manner. "Then you could keep the ones you want and tear up or burn the ones you don't."

"You're being melodramatic about this."

"*I'm* being melodramatic?" Rie scoffed. She was already over it. All of it. And that was why she could laugh and joke about it at the very end like this. "I'm acting just the same as always."

"Hey, what kind of lunch did you pack for me?" Minoru asked after suddenly closing the album.

"I can't tell you. Wouldn't want to ruin the surprise. Anyway, you need to get going. It's a three-hour drive to Okayama, right? You need to get going if you wanna beat the traffic."

"It's not like I have to be there at a specific time. Besides, eating lunch all alone at a rest stop in my car is just—"

"What's wrong with you? You're the one who asked me to pack you a lunch because you were driving all the way to Okayama."

"I know, but…think of how lonely I'd be if I ate this lunch all by myself."

"Hiroko is waiting for you in Okayama. Is she not? She and her family are all at her house waiting for you. They want to have that wedding already. How long has it been? Four months?"

"Five months," Minoru pointed out in naive honesty.

"Oh my. Then you really should hurry up with the wedding before people start to wonder. Are your parents not coming?"

"I think my sister'll be there."

"Oh, so you've already talked about it with them?"

"It was sudden. Everything's been really hectic."

"You don't need to explain yourself. It doesn't bother me." She slightly tilted her head to the side out of habit.

Rie had high cheekbones and a long face, which made her appear stern or lonely at times, but she knew she was beautiful depending on how you looked at her. Rie was shameless in this regard and had a very high opinion of herself, more than anyone might expect.

"If you say so. Anyway, let's eat that lunch you made together."

"But…"

"Come on."

Minoru began unwrapping his lunch box, so Rie decided to put up some tea to go with it. They had already signed and submitted their divorce papers but were still living together, since the construction being done on Minoru's new apartment in Kyoto was taking longer than expected, and he had been taking forever to finish packing. He said he was leaving today, so this was going to be their last day together.

"All right. This is our last day together, so we might as well."

"Last this, last that—stop saying 'last' so much." Minoru seemed to relax the moment Rie decided to join him for lunch. "I can leave for Okayama tomorrow, you know. Stay another night here," he said.

"No, you can't. Do you know what they'd say if you did that? If you don't want to go to Okayama today, then go to your apartment in Kyoto and stay there. You don't want to give anyone the wrong idea."

"Nobody has to know."

"I don't want you staying here."

Rie began making another bowl of soup. After opening his lunch box, Minoru rubbed his hands together with evident satisfaction.

"Meatballs... Nice," he muttered.

Inside the lunch box were soft simmered meatballs in seasoned broth, pickled lotus root with fried eggs (Minoru loved these fried eggs, so they were a must with every lunch), white rice with black sesame seasoning, and Minoru's favorite chopped vegetables pickled in salt with red *shiso* leaves. Rie had made herself the same thing. Minoru let out a satisfied sigh after seeing the two lunches together, then grabbed his lacquered lunch box and began busily stuffing his chopsticks into it.

His appetite was as strong as ever. Minoru wasn't a drinker, but he was a big eater. He loved food, and he especially loved the food that Rie cooked.

Rie had spent the past ten years working for a company that made and distributed women's clothing. Things had been extremely busy ever since she was assigned to sales. She often went to boutiques and warehouses on business trips, and she had to make frequent trips to fashion shows and department stores while meeting with designers in between. Most of the time, the week was over before she even realized it.

Once a week, she had to have dinner meetings with coworkers and clients, but even then, she went back home first to make Minoru his dinner. It wasn't as if Rie was an exceptional cook or anything; she just knew exactly what Minoru liked and what he needed, so she would be hit with new ideas for dinner left and right, which he seemed to greatly enjoy.

"I can't eat out when dinner at home is this good. Nothing beats your cooking," he used to say.

"This is delicious… I can't even imagine not getting to eat your cooking anymore. I can come over to eat sometimes, right?" Minoru asked as he ate the lunch Rie had made for him.

"You've got to be kidding me. What is wrong with you? There's no reason for you to come here anymore. Besides, I'm planning on moving anyway."

"You are? You never told me that." He seemed flustered. His droopy eyes widened. "I mean, not telling me is kind of a mean thing to do. Don't you think?"

"You're the mean one, suddenly dropping all that on me and surprising me out of nowhere."

"Yeah… Sorry about that."

Minoru gulped. Rie didn't want to keep blaming him for what happened. They had been married for eight years until…

"Hey, I didn't wanna have to tell you this, but things have gotten a little complicated with a female customer from work."

Never once did she expect to ever hear him say that.

"She said she didn't want to live anymore if I didn't marry her," he admitted in a dumbfounded manner while he scratched his head.

"Well, that's a little extreme. Why'd she say that?"

Rie wanted to complain to Minoru that day because she had some trouble at work, but he dropped the next few words on her the moment she got home, making her recoil in astonishment.

"She told me she's pregnant."

Rie sucked in a deep breath, and Minoru averted his gaze.

"I'm sorry," he said. "After debating day after day when I should tell you, the time just flew by."

"..."

"What should I do?"

Rie unconsciously glared at him in a reprimanding way.

"I'm sorry," Minoru squeaked again.

Even when he apologized, his drooping eyes and baby face made it look like he was half smiling. Minoru was hanging his head slightly—perhaps he was expecting to be yelled at—but Rie was so taken aback that she couldn't even get a word out. The gloves she was trying to take off got tangled up because her hands were trembling. What Minoru said shocked her as if she'd been sprayed in the face with ink. Minoru wasn't a liar, but hiding something was even worse than lying about it.

"She told me she's pregnant."

She would never be able to wash that ink off her face. The abruptness of it all made her feel that way even more strongly. The ink had flown all over the place, staining every part of her mind and body in the hardest places to clean.

Rie spent their entire eight-year marriage unable to have a child. Not that she wasn't capable, however. The doctor even told her it was possible for her to get pregnant, but for some reason, she couldn't. Time went by, and her and Minoru's lives as a double income, no-kids household was fulfilling and enjoyable.

"Maybe we don't need to have a child?"

"Yeah, I don't really even want one," Minoru had replied, and with that, the whole idea vanished from Rie's life.

Which was why the first thing that popped into her head when she heard about the pregnancy was confusion:

We already crossed that bridge. We put that topic to bed long ago, and yet you want to try again?

"What do you plan on doing?"

"I don't know what I should do. My sister—"

"Oh, you already told your sister?"

"Yeah, and she told me to talk it over with her. Her being the other woman, not you."

Minoru's parents had already passed away, so his sister and her husband were like parents to him. Rie, however, didn't like his sister. She'd been against the idea of her brother marrying a woman three years his senior from day one. Minoru and Rie worked at the same company, so Rie ended up quitting when they married and found a new job. But...

"She's never going to be able to have a child if she keeps working like that," Minoru's sister once said to him. And slowly but surely, Minoru's attitude of "not even really wanting one" changed.

"I'm sorry, Rie...but I want a kid now just like everyone else," Minoru eventually admitted. Rie could just tell it was his sister who put him up to this. It was the way he said it that made it clear she had poisoned his mind.

"...How old is she?" Rie asked, her voice slightly hoarse.

"Twenty-three."

"What's her name?"

"Hiroko Ohara."

"Do you like her?"

"I don't know if I'd go that far, but she's funny and fun to be around."

Rie settled into a chair in silence, still wearing her work clothes. She couldn't even joke about this. If she had just a little bit more energy, she would have probably been able to at least respond to what was happening, but the depression had already kicked in. Tears of self-pity began welling in her eyes and she suddenly got the urge to throw up.

And yet all it took was a single word to tease those feelings out.

"Dinner," Minoru suddenly said. Rie thought she was hearing things.

"What?"

"Let's eat. I'm starving."

"I don't care. Make your own dinner if it means that much to you!"

"What are we having tonight?"

Whether lightning struck, whether spears fell from the sky, whether it came out that Minoru was cheating on her, he still seemed to expect that she would make dinner for him. That was just how faithful his healthy, blinding ego was to his desires and his desires alone. Apparently, the reason he told Rie the truth wasn't because of any moral obligation or guilt. He simply couldn't take the weight of keeping a secret any longer.

Rie's resentful tears dried up along with her tears of self-pity. She didn't have an appetite. She was fed up. She got in bed and tried to process the insanity, but nothing helped. A twenty-three-year-old woman said she didn't want to be alive if Minoru didn't marry her, and Minoru said she was fun to be around. Rie didn't know how to even wrap her head around that. She was at a loss. Minoru had always been rather popular with the ladies, something Rie used to be able to laugh and joke about at the dinner table, but she never expected for things to go this far.

Before she even realized it, she started feeling pain in her neck and fingers. She'd been curled up in bed with her big jewelry on still. Rie had a large frame, so every jewel she had was similarly large, and yet she still forgot to remove them.

Minoru peeked into the room.

"Hey...," he timidly squeaked. "Um... Where's the salt-flavored ramen?"

"Shut up!"

Rie was genuinely repulsed by Minoru in that moment. She jumped out of bed, then immediately threw the magazine by the bedside at him. It was so sudden that Minoru was unable to dodge in time, and it hit him in the chest.

"You don't have to throw a fit like that...," he muttered feebly.

Rie rarely got angry. In fact, this was the first time she'd lost her temper since they got married, so the pupils in his drooping, now furtive eyes shrank. Rie was always a kind woman who never showed anger or insulted others, so it must have been quite the shock for him.

"Geez. You're scaring me," he said, but that still didn't put her in a better mood, so he narrowed his eyes and got mad back at her. "I should be the angry one. You seriously didn't buy more ramen when you were at the store?"

He got grumpy when he was hungry. Rie had felt a rage burning in her stomach, but the moment she heard him say that, the anger suddenly left her body. Minoru always proved to have a screw loose at times like this, which Rie usually found amusing, but today, she immediately lost all energy to argue and listlessly replied:

"The ramen's on the second shelf from the top."

"Why didn't you cry earlier?" Minoru asked later on. "You would've melted my heart with that pretty face of yours if you did."

"Would you have changed your mind about leaving if I did?"

"I don't know about that," came his honest reply.

"Then crying would've been pointless," Rie said with a laugh.

She was annoyed, but she couldn't cry or beg. She couldn't use her tears to get what she wanted. She couldn't do something that was pointless, and there was nothing she could do about Minoru, who had a screw loose.

Now that she thought about it, maybe this Hiroko Ohara woman was a good match for him. Now that she was further along in her pregnancy, she'd apparently left her job and started working at a boutique near Sanjo Keihan Station in Kyoto. When Rie said she wanted to meet her, Minoru immediately called Hiroko up and asked her to meet Rie at the café across from the Kabuki theater.

It was a cold day with signs of snow in the sky, but she energetically walked right into the café in high spirits. Hiroko's eyes were round, and her lips were round and full as well. She seemed bubbly.

She took off her faux-leather coat, revealing her unbleached, thick cotton loose-fitting jacket and pants of the same color, along with a brown velvet belt loosely tied. Her stomach didn't stand out at all, perhaps due to her clothes.

"I'm Hiroko Ohara. You're Minoru's wife, right? He showed me your picture," she said, unprompted. When she spoke, her lips made her look youthful like a little girl. Rie had thought about what she was going to say to her when they finally met, but she felt they weren't the right words for a girl like Hiroko and immediately forgot what she wanted to say. Instead, her inner saleswoman kicked in and she asked curiously:

"I like your outfit. Where did you get it?"

"At the Tik Tak in America Mura in Osaka when they were on sale. They've got a Tik Tak here in Kyoto now, too, though. Right behind this place. I can take you there later if you want. They've got a ton of nice clothes."

"Oh, I heard their clothes have gotten a lot nicer lately. Like a total rebranding."

"Yeah, their style's kind of similar to Mon Ami's now, but way cooler."

"Are you from Kyoto?"

"No, I was born in Okayama, but I went to high school in Kyoto and have been living here ever since."

She sounded like she wanted to talk more about fashion, making it unclear why she even came to meet Rie in the first place. And yet with a smile on her face, she said:

"I decided to work at a boutique because I wanted to see pretty things and get excited about them. I thought it might be good for the baby, you know?"

She rubbed her stomach.

"'Good for the baby'?" Rie repeated.

"Yeah, they say babies can hear noises outside the womb. If you fight or get mad or yell or say something mean, they'll come out with a twisted personality."

There was no way Rie could start a fight or insult Hiroko now.

"How do your parents feel about all this?"

It took everything she had to ask that.

"They were surprised at first, but I keep telling them I'm gonna have the baby no matter what. I plan on going back home after things cool off a little. My mom said she already booked a hospital."

Hiroko was treating the entire situation like she was talking about Tik Tak again.

"I'll have the cream parfait and some juice," she then told the waiter. It could snow at any minute in this cold weather, and yet she was going to eat something cold.

Only a young person could do that. I'm impressed, thought Rie. Hiroko began licking her spoon and talking in between bites of her parfait.

"You should have a baby, too, before it's too late. They say it's hard for older women to get pregnant, let alone raise a child. The doctor told me I'm at the best age to have a baby."

She wasn't saying this out of spite or sarcastically. She was speaking joyfully from the heart. Once again, all the tension left Rie's body. She felt ridiculous even trying to humor Hiroko. Common sense and manners were an afterthought to this girl. It was as if giving birth to a healthy baby was simply something fashionable to her, just like wearing clothes from Tik Tak.

"That's wonderful. I hope you give birth to a very healthy baby," Rie replied. She felt compelled to say that even though she didn't want to.

She left without saying anything mean because that would be bad for the baby, but when she stepped outside, she found the streets of Gion in the middle of a blizzard. Only a few moments went by until she was covered in snow, and the freezing tip of her nose had turned red. She wondered what she did to have to suffer like this, and as the tips of her toes slowly grew colder, she felt a pang in her bladder.

Rie had chronic cystitis, so this occasionally happened when she got cold. She clutched her lower abdomen in pain as the snow continued piling up. At this point, the discomfort was more than just a pang. Her bladder was inflamed, and she was miserable. After squatting under the eaves of a building, she wondered whether she should run into the nearest café, when…

"Hey, are you okay?" came a friendly voice. It was Hiroko Ohara, the girl she was just talking to in the café. "I work just over there. There's a sofa, so how about stopping by to warm up your feet and relax? Your feet are gonna freeze in those high heels. And then you won't be able to have children if that happens."

That annoyed Rie because she knew there was no malice behind those cheerful words. Regardless, she took Hiroko up on her offer and lay down on the sofa as the kindly female boutique owner brought a heater, placed it by her feet, and made her some hot tea. Only then did Rie finally feel relief. The snow eventually began coming down harder and more fiercely.

"Looks like we're closing early today… We should hurry home before they close the station from all the snow. Hiroko, you're free to go. I'll be heading out, too, in a second," the owner said.

Rie had Hiroko get Minoru for her. His workplace was very close to Kyoto, and with this much snow, it was pretty clear that the Meishin Expressway was going to be closed off, so Rie wouldn't be able to take a taxi home. Her only choice was to have Minoru walk her to the station and take the train back with her. Minoru showed up at the boutique around an hour after Hiroko called him.

"Thank you for taking care of her. I really appreciate it."

While he may not have been the sharpest tool in the shed, he still made sure to thank the owner.

"You should thank Hiroko, too, for all the trouble you've caused her," Rie said despite herself.

Hiroko had bought some disposable heating pads at the local convenience store, which she'd placed on Rie's lower abdomen for her to warm her up. She was surprisingly thoughtful and observant, maybe because she'd once worked as an office clerk.

"I'm really sorry about all this," Minoru told Hiroko.

"Take care of yourself," she said to Rie. Her voice was excessively cheerful.

"Why did I even want to meet her in the first place?" Rie murmured to herself. However, after a week went by, she showed up at the boutique with a box of cakes as a thank-you. Another girl was working there that day instead of Hiroko—a slim lady who obviously wasn't pregnant.

"Oh, Hiroko went back to her hometown to see her family. She needed to start resting and preparing for the baby." It was the chatty owner, wearing very fashionable light-violet glasses. "She told me you were her husband's sister…"

He was already being called her husband.

The lunch box's meatballs were very rich in flavor, different from Western or Japanese ones. They could even be eaten cold, they were so rich. The chef herself—Rie—also thought they were good, so it was no surprise when Minoru scarfed them down. There were even fried eggs, which made him more than satisfied.

Rie used to think that only she knew how to cook for Minoru, since she knew exactly what he liked, and that there was no way someone young like Hiroko could make anything worthwhile (Rie wasn't trying to use her cooking to keep him from leaving her, though). But lately, she'd started thinking that Minoru could and would eat anything with great enthusiasm while repeating how delicious it was.

Perhaps it didn't matter who cooked for him, and perhaps Hiroko, with her bubbly personality, was only joking when she said she would die if Minoru didn't marry her. After realizing that, it was like the last weight had been removed from Rie's shoulders, instantly relaxing her. Her heart stopped racing, and her vague anxiety and jealousy faded as well—just like her cystitis.

Even when Minoru said he was going to Okayama tomorrow...

"Uh-huh," Rie casually replied, even though she knew he was going to Hiroko's family's home.

"Pack me a lunch, will ya?"

"Okay."

"I plan on stopping at a rest area along the way, so I'll eat it then."

"Why don't you just eat the food they have there?"

"Because I want to eat your cooking."

Rie knew that after he returned from Okayama, he would be coming home with Hiroko as his new wife and moving into their apartment in Kyoto. She knew this, but she still made him a lunch, since this was going to be the last time she ever would. For the most part, they decided to split their furniture and household goods down the middle, but...

"Rie, you can keep whatever you want. We should take the things we want most."

"There isn't anything I want."

Rie suddenly remembered an old story she once read. A wife whose husband was about to leave her was told to bring whatever she wanted with her when she moved out.

"What would I need when I'm leaving behind the only thing

that has ever meant anything to me: you?" the woman asked with a smile.

Right as she was about to leave emptyhanded, her husband stopped her. He was so touched by her words that he changed his mind. They got back together and lived happily ever after.

But saying something like that to Minoru would be pointless. Seeing Minoru leave, with his half of the Ginori coffee cups and photos of himself, merely emphasized the absurdity of it all. He wasn't leaving emptyhanded.

"You really should get going. It's dangerous to drive on the expressway at night," Rie told him.

"Yeah... What are you gonna do after I'm gone?"

"Hmm... I think I'm going to continue working at the same company."

"No, no, no. I meant: How are you going to spend the rest of your Sunday night?"

"Read a few magazines, I suppose."

There were a lot of trade and fashion magazines she needed to look through for information on boutiques and the like. In fact, her job kept her far busier than an ordinary office worker like Minoru.

"Hey, Rie," he muttered absentmindedly. "Make sure you get cystitis every once in a while."

"Why?"

"Because I'll come see you. Call me and tell me you need me, and I'll be here."

"Ha-ha-ha!" Rie cackled. "You're going to make me have second thoughts if you say such sweet things to me."

"Really? Maybe I should leave tomorrow, then?"

"No. I was just trying to be nice."

She didn't even see him off. After about an hour went by, he called her.

"How's your bladder? Feeling inflamed yet?"

"Actually, I feel great. Better than I've felt in a long time now that I'm alone."

"Looks like I'm not needed. Well, anyway, take care. I've just reached Yamazaki."

There was a note of disappointment in Minoru's voice, even more so than when he'd been there with her. He was undoubtedly despondent, clutching the steering wheel with uneasiness in his drooping eyes.

And it wasn't without reason. After all, he was about to be taken prisoner. He was going to be held captive by a little something called family.

Rie, who had escaped that fate and was finally able to relax, strongly felt that way. Not having anyone to call when she was having bladder problems might be rough for a little while, but for whatever reason, she felt a release like no other.

Rie poured more coffee into her Ginori mug.

I should've given him these last two sets of coffee cups, too, she thought.

Being let go helped her let go of any attachments she once had as well.

Josee, the Tiger and the Fish

"Wow! Look at that bridge!"

"Wow! Look, the ocean!"

Josee shouted with joy until she was out of breath. (She had difficulty breathing sometimes, especially when she laughed too much or the wind blew right in her face. It felt as if she were being robbed of oxygen. This apparently had something to do with the fact that she was paralyzed from the waist down, although Josee herself didn't really understand it. She'd been diagnosed with cerebral palsy as a child, but then another doctor said, "This is completely different from CP. She doesn't have any of the classic symptoms." Eventually, her doctors just settled on a cerebral palsy diagnosis and called it a day. Josee never really got any concrete answers about her condition, even now, at twenty-five years old.)

The wind blew right in her face, so she started choking. She tried to shout, but the wind drowned her out.

"Josee, close the window already! What, you like not being able to breathe or something?" said Tsuneo. Josee hurriedly pressed a button by the seat and closed the car window.

The last car they'd rented had a handle you needed to crank to open and close the windows. That was really hard on Josee, depending on the position of the handles, so she was thrilled to be in a car that had windows she could control with the press of a button. One press got her excited, so she pressed it several more times.

Tsuneo chided her good-naturedly: "Quit playing with the switch."

"I've never seen anything so amazing...," Josee muttered with evident mirth.

"There's cars out there with even better features."

"I'm talking about this trip. I've never seen scenery this beautiful before."

"This is my first time here, too."

"Don't even try to compare your first time with mine. This is a way bigger deal for me. It's only the second time I've ever seen the ocean."

"Yeah, yeah. Brag all you want. Still the first honeymoon for the both of us."

"Heh-heh."

"Ever gone on a trip with anyone before, Josee?"

"I'll just leave that to your imagination. I was very popular back in the day, unlike you, Caretaker."

"Tsk."

Josee only called Tsuneo Caretaker when she was in an especially good mood.

One day, Tsuneo had stepped into the bathroom before they went out. "Gimme a second," he said.

"Stop. I didn't say you could pee! Who do you think you are?! Get outta there!" Josee yelled from outside the door, clearly irritated.

"The heck's wrong with you? Is that any way to talk to your husband?" Tsuneo said as he finished up.

"You're not my husband!"

"Then what am I?"

"My caretaker!"

Josee had just said the first thing that came to mind, but she actually took a liking to it, and from then on, she started occasionally calling Tsuneo Caretaker. Sometimes, Tsuneo would preface his own opinions with, "As your caretaker, I think…" He was very flexible in that sense and could easily adapt to anything. He even started calling Josee "Josee" after she suddenly asked him to call her that.

"From now on, my name is Josee," she declared one day, seemingly out of nowhere.

"How'd you get from Kumi to Josee?" Tsuneo looked puzzled.

"No reason. But Josee suits me better. I'm retiring the name Kumi."

"I don't think you can change your name that easily. No city hall or authority is gonna call you that."

"I don't care what the government thinks. All that matters is that I wanna be called Josee, so that's how you're gonna refer to me from now on."

After some prodding, Tsuneo learned that Josee loved novels and often borrowed some from city hall's mobile library (people with disabilities didn't have to pay a membership fee to borrow books) which was how she became familiar with the works of Françoise Sagan. Josee had picked out one of Sagan's books, thinking it was a mystery novel, but after reading it, she became hooked and read several more by the author.

Sagan had a habit of naming the heroines in her novels Josée, which Josee immediately fell in love with. She thought the name Josee Yamamura sounded so much better than Kumiko Yamamura. She felt as if the name were calling her, telling her something good would happen—no—that something good had *already* happened, and that good thing was Tsuneo coming into her life.

Tsuneo said that Josee was a weird name (he didn't read too many novels, and he didn't associate the name with anything when he said it), but after spending so much time together, he eventually started calling her Josee as well.

Josee sometimes adopted quirks of the singers she watched on TV, but this was the first time a name had ever made such an impact on her. She'd always had a strong personality, though. When her father remarried, his new wife moved in and brought her three-year-old daughter along. Josee's father doted on the little girl. When Josee was fourteen years old, she started acting out in an attempt to get her father's love and attention as well. But once she needed a wheelchair to get around and started her period, Josee became a burden to her stepmother, who sent her to an assisted living facility. Her father had visited from time to time at first, but he soon stopped coming altogether. Josee's tough persona still stuck with her, regardless.

She didn't remember her mother, since her mother left when Josee was a baby. At seventeen, she was adopted by her paternal grandmother and started living with her in the suburbs. Her grandmother was very kind, but she was too embarrassed to have people see Josee in a wheelchair, so she took her out only at night. Josee's grandmother would gently bring her through the back door, but she was a frail old woman, so she was never that good at pushing the wheelchair around. Nevertheless, Josee still badly wanted to go out at night in the spring and summer.

One time when the two of them went out, they passed a store that hadn't yet closed. "Give me just a second," her grandmother said, then went inside to do a little shopping—detergent, toilet paper, that sort of thing. Josee was just outside the store, not far from her grandmother, but the street was on a slight incline. One side had a long fenced-in yard and was dark from the tree cover.

Josee briefly sensed someone nearby, and the next thing she knew, her wheelchair started moving. It was only later on that she realized the presence she felt was spite. Tsuneo once said it was probably just some drunk messing around, but Josee didn't think so. While she was living in the assisted living facility, she became highly sensitive to spiteful presences.

A man passing by had pushed Josee's wheelchair down the hill without warning before running away. The wheelchair slid down the hill at full tilt. Josee's grandmother chased after her, screaming bloody murder, but Josee was so shaken up at the time that she didn't remember. All she knew was that some stranger had shoved her wheelchair and that she had sensed his malicious intent. There was nothing she could do except scream.

Her shrieking startled a nearby man, who saw the wheelchair hurtling down the hill and threw himself in front of it. He was standing right at the bottom of the hill, which ended in a gentle curve. The impact knocked him to the ground, stopping the wheelchair's descent.

"Are you okay?" the man asked as he quickly got to his feet.

Josee, meanwhile, was in a daze and couldn't say anything. Getting worked up made it difficult for her to breathe, so she was desperately trying to take steady breaths. She looked dead lying there on the ground, so the man apparently started panicking, but it was all one big racket to Josee. Only after hearing her grandmother's voice as she came rushing down the hill was Josee able to calm down.

"I can't believe someone would do such a thing," the man said, still quite agitated. He then offered to take Josee home in case whoever had pushed her was still around. The man who caught Josee at the bottom of the hill was Tsuneo, a college student at the time, who'd been living in a nearby off-campus apartment.

Ever since then, he would show up at Josee's house whenever he was free and help her get around. Josee's body had never fully developed, so she was very petite, which was why Tsuneo always thought she was younger than him.

"Kumi, you're either totally clueless, or you know everything there is to know. There's no middle ground with you," he once told her. He was surprised, however, to learn that she was actually two years older than him. Tsuneo was right, though. There were a lot of things Josee was totally clueless about, since she'd spent so long cooped up in either an assisted living facility or her home. She never joined any clubs or activist groups for the disabled, so she never met any new people. Josee was something of a wallflower, always shy and anxious around the facility's young volunteers. They started avoiding her, until one day, she ended up completely by the wayside.

All her knowledge had come from reading or the TV.

"I used to play in this huge yard that had a swing set and a pond with dozens of koi swimmin' in it. My old house was massive," she'd boasted to Tsuneo. However, those were things she'd seen in books and on television. She'd never attended school, since she was exempt from enrollment, although her father had taught her how to read and write katakana, hiragana, and kanji. She learned the rest of her kanji from books and her ABCs from English-language fairy tales people had given her.

Josee also played a lot of shogi with her father, since he taught her the rules. When her father was at work, she would listen to baseball games on the radio. He'd taught her about baseball, too, but she wanted to see a real game so badly that she ended up having him carry her on his back to watch one in person. It was at Koshien Stadium, and she got to see the pitcher Murayama. She also vaguely remembered spying the shortstop Yoshida, whom she really liked. Her memories of the games she saw on TV, the ones she heard on the radio, and the game she saw in person with her father were all jumbled together in the back of her mind.

"It rained during the second half, but he put his jacket over me so I wouldn't get wet."

That was another memory Josee shared with Tsuneo, but in truth, she'd actually been watching that game on the TV at her assisted living facility. The skies opened up, and the fans in the stands frantically covered their heads with newspapers and coats. It left such a strong impression on Josee that it got jumbled together with the childhood memory of her and her father seeing a baseball game in person.

"My dad was a real nice man, y'know. He'd do whatever I asked," Josee bragged.

But then Tsuneo teased, "If he was so nice, why'd he send you to that facility?"

"Shut up! Fuck you, asshole! Like I give a shit about that."

She was furious to the point that she almost started having trouble breathing again, so Tsuneo kept his mouth shut. That was when he realized: Josee wasn't lying as much as she was saying what she wished were true. These were her dreams, and while they weren't real, they were an undeniable part of who she was.

Josee and her grandmother were on welfare, but they could sometimes splurge enough to treat a poor college student like Tsuneo to dinner. He lived off instant ramen whenever he was in between part-time jobs, so Josee's grandmother's home cooking was like heaven. There would be tofu with konjak and spinach and miso soup and so many other treats. Sometimes, she would cook old-people food like squid and radish boiled in soy sauce, but those only added to Tsuneo's delight. Soon, he started spending more and more of his days at the pair's quiet homestead.

"What's this mean?" Josee would ask Tsuneo when she didn't understand something she had read. Josee couldn't walk, but her upper body was just as strong as an able-bodied person's. She didn't like listening to tapes of volunteers reading aloud to people who were permanently bedridden; she wanted to read books for herself. That said, listening to the tapes would be much less work...

Tsuneo wasn't so much tripped up by Josee's bookworm tendencies but rather at a loss for what to do about her domineering personality. His college degree had absolutely nothing to do with social welfare, so he had no clue about working with people with disabilities.

Tsuneo consulted a friend who had experience as a volunteer caretaker. He told Tsuneo that many in the disabled community could be combative because of all the discrimination they faced, and that commonly made them come off as abrasive. But Tsuneo didn't feel like that applied to Josee. She hated doing anything in big groups and wasn't the type to pressure the local government through protests or demonstrations. Far from it, she led a very quiet, private life.

Some of that had to do with her grandmother's reluctance to let her leave the house. She didn't want Josee running into any bill collectors or people working for the city.

Josee's only access to the outside world was Tsuneo. He took her to a bathhouse far away (at around eleven PM when it was about to close and the owner didn't mind her coming in) and once she finished, he picked her up off the floor and put her in her wheelchair, then hopped over to the men's bath for a soak. He figured he might as well while he was there.

"The hell do you think you're doing, making me wait in the cold? I'm freezin' out here."

Josee chided him while she waited for him to finish up his bath.

"What did I do to deserve being treated like that?" Tsuneo mumbled as he pushed her back to the car. But for all his complaining, he had a feeling that her haughtiness might be due to her emotional dependency. They were two sides of the same coin. However, he knew saying that would only make her furious or cause her to have trouble breathing, so he kept it to himself. Tsuneo was neither used to nor capable of analyzing and articulating the intricacies of the human psyche.

He'd never met a woman like Josee, whose beautiful doll-like features belied such a filthy mouth. All the girls on campus were shameless and bold like a pack of tigresses. They had this sexual energy to them. Josee, on the other hand, wasn't particularly enticing, and Tsuneo always felt like he had stolen an old doll out of the cellar whenever he accompanied her. But her brash attitude suited her to a T.

All the homes in Josee's neighborhood still had outhouses, but once the sewage system was up and running, the city's welfare division gave Josee's grandmother a subsidy, which they used to get a modernized toilet. They were even able to get a footstool installed around the toilet and safety rails to make things easier for Josee. It was Tsuneo's job to relay Josee's thoughts about the new toilet's design to the contractors.

She complained relentlessly, telling him the footstool was too high or the safety rails were too low. Tsuneo would then ask the contractors directly, "Hey, sorry, but do you think you could make some adjustments to these?"

Josee's grandmother was already in her eighties by this point, so staying on her feet was becoming too much of a hassle for her, even in the kitchen. Josee decided to take over, but the counter was too high, and that made cooking in a wheelchair extremely difficult. Tsuneo liked building things, so eventually, he made her a table, installed a shelf, and gradually fixed up the old house until the kitchen was wheelchair accessible. Josee had a bevy of tough requests, and Tsuneo would get fed up from time to time.

"You don't honestly think I can do something that complicated, do you?" he'd tell her. But they didn't have enough money to hire a professional, so they had no other choice but to make do with Tsuneo's amateur skills.

Josee could cook, albeit very slowly. She took her time cutting vegetables that made for excellent stews. She could do laundry as well and had no issue using the laundry bar Tsuneo modified for her. Josee could hold herself up on crutches, so while she still couldn't go outside on her own, she could at least get around the house more easily. One of the sets of crutches Tsuneo made was shaped like a snowshoe at the bottom to prevent Josee from falling. The other set, which Josee called her roller skates, was fashioned from two poles stuck into half an old vacuum cleaner he'd found in a junkyard. Whenever Josee leaned into the poles, the casters on the bottom of the vacuum sent her rolling forward. One time, she almost threw herself off the porch by accident.

Tsuneo didn't spend every waking minute at Josee's house, though. He made the most of his college days, went on vacations, visited family back in his hometown near Hiroshima, and enjoyed skiing. Finally, it came time to graduate, and he started panicking when his job search didn't bear fruit, which kept him from going over to Josee's house for a little while. Eventually, he landed a municipal job in one of the smaller neighboring towns. But when he visited Josee's place for the first time in a long while, a different family had moved in.

"The old lady who used to live here died, and her handicapped granddaughter started living on welfare in the apartment up the street. She's apparently on her own," they told him.

He immediately went searching for the apartment until he found one with a wheelchair sitting outside, covered in a plastic sheet to protect it from the rain. When he knocked on the door, the person to answer was none other than Josee, a snowshoe crutch under one arm and a roller skate one under the other.

Her appearance, however, caught his attention the most. She was even skinnier than before. Her chin was more pointed, and her eyes looked bigger. Her hair was still cut in a bob, but it had lost its sheen, something Tsuneo attributed to malnutrition. He was never under any obligation to periodically check in on Josee, but he nonetheless found himself racked with guilt.

"Sorry. I've been really busy lately," he said. "Had so much on my plate that I couldn't find time to stop by. Forgive me. I heard your grandmother died?"

"Yeah," Josee replied. She didn't seem as depressed as he thought she would be, and he could tell from her eyes that she wasn't about to scold him. Josee had a very sharp tongue, so Tsuneo thought she was going to yell at him and blame him or at least complain about her grandmother's death, but she was surprisingly calm and expressionless.

"People from the city gave her a funeral," she explained. "Getting an apartment was a bigger pain in the ass, though. Hard to find a place that has cheap rent and no stairs."

"Are you really living on your own?"

"This volunteer lady comes by once a month, does all my shopping for me."

"…Are your neighbors at least nice?"

"Nah, they don't even give me the time of day. Probably just trying not to cause me any trouble. Doesn't help that there's this really creepy old man who lives on the second floor, though. Said he'd do anything for me if I let him touch my tits. You should've seen the nasty grin on his face. I'm too freaked out to go anywhere at night, so I just stay home. Daytime's fine, though, since he's usually out watching speedboat racing or bike racing then."

It was the first time Tsuneo got to talk to Josee in what seemed like forever, but she sounded very detached. That was when he realized that Josee had been down and out ever since she lost her grandmother. Seeing her like this was so depressing that Tsuneo pretended to look around her apartment just to hide the pain he was in. Josee had apparently sold her grandmother's chest, dresser, and alcove shelves, among other things, to be able to make rent.

"All I've got is whatever's in these boxes, but it's fine, since I can move everything around by myself. I've been snatching up any clean cardboard boxes I find in town."

Josee had swiped some fashion magazines from a dentist's waiting room, then cut out the colorful illustrations and glued them onto the cardboard boxes she had piled on top of one another. She'd even fashioned the boxes into drawers that opened when she pulled on the ends. For all she lacked in the way of belongings, these boxes upon multicolored boxes filled her tiny apartment to capacity.

"Have you been eating? You look like you've lost a lot of weight. Your face is thinner and kind of shriveled up."

"Don't you dare pity me. Yeah, I'm eating. I'm doing just fine!" she barked while turning her head away and scowling.

Tsuneo wasn't thinking before he spoke, and he seemed to have offended her and her big ego as a result. It wasn't until he'd known Josee for a while that Tsuneo noticed how she liked her smooth, snow-white skin and her small yet well-proportioned doll-like features. She truly considered herself drop-dead gorgeous, so it upset her when Tsuneo said her face looked "shriveled up."

He got to his feet as if he'd had enough of Josee's ranting.

"I'll stop by again sometime," he said.

"Don't bother! I don't want you comin' here anymore!" Josee shouted.

"...All right. Bye."

He didn't have any other choice but to leave. He started putting on his sneakers at the front door, when...

"Where do you think you're going?! You plan on leaving after upsetting me like this?!"

Josee was out of breath.

"What do you want me to do?" he asked.

"I don't know!"

"...Bye, then."

All of a sudden, the snowshoe-shaped crutch hit him in the back. Tsuneo turned around to find tears welling in Josee's big eyes.

"Kumi," he said.

"Hurry up and go. Get out of here... And never come back!" Josee hollered, still teary-eyed. She was hysterical, desperately trying to breathe. Tsuneo couldn't leave her like this. He cautiously approached her.

"I don't want you to go," Josee wailed before clinging to him. "Please don't go. At least stay for another thirty minutes. I sold the TV, and the radio's broken, and I'm just...so lonely..."

"Wait. So I'm just a replacement for your TV and radio?"

"Yep. I like you better than my last radio, though, since you can talk back." Josee laughed through her tears, and that instantly reminded Tsuneo how cute she was. Those unbelievably tiny, beautiful lips of hers were right in front of him, so he went ahead and kissed her. After he'd held her tensed lips in his for a few moments, her mouth gradually opened, and he immediately trapped her warm, small tongue before it could escape.

The only noise outside the quiet apartment was the revving of a motorcycle.

"You can do anything you want to me, Tsuneo. Anything," Josee said once she eventually took her lips off his. Her breath was ragged.

"Like what?"

"*Like what*? I know you wanna do me."

"No, I don't. I'm not like that creep on the second floor."

"Do you hate me or something?"

"...I don't hate you," he was forced to say.

"Then let's do it. C'mon, what kind of man are you?"

"...That's not why I came all the way here."

"Oh, shut up. It's not like I was planning on doing any of this today, either, but now I want to. Plus, I like you. I would never say something like this to anyone else. I don't know where this is gonna go, but I've never felt this way before."

"You're sure about this?"

"Is the door locked?"

"No, it's not."

She immediately made Tsuneo lock it. Just like always, Josee was forcing him into things. This wasn't going to be his first time with a woman, either. He'd slept with a few classmates in the past, but never anyone so seemingly fragile.

It wasn't until that day that he'd ever seen Josee's slim legs up close; they reminded him of a doll's. And though her body was as exquisite as one would expect from a doll, as far as he could tell, her feminine functions seemed quite healthy and robust. Josee had learned about sex from TV and magazines to an extent, but somewhere in the process, she appeared to stop pretending to know what she was doing. She was at a loss for words and in a daze, even when Tsuneo finished.

"Are you mad…?" he whispered into Josee's ear as he sat up and held her in his arms.

"I'm not mad," she replied quietly yet matter-of-factly. "It was just totally different than how I imagined it'd be."

"In a bad way?"

"In a good way."

"…Glad to hear it."

Tsuneo thought back to the flings he'd had with the women he met at school, many of whom he had no interest in seeing again once they'd slept together. But here Josee (he'd still called her Kumi back in college) was pressed up against him, and he never wanted this moment to end.

"I like you. And I like what you do, too," said Josee, which Tsuneo found adorable. "Stay the night."

"Okay."

"And tomorrow. All day, all night."

"I have a job, so I gotta go to work. You know how that creep on the second floor is out at the boat races during the day? Well, all men are like that. We all have to work during the day."

"If you don't do what I say, I'm gonna tell everyone you forced yourself on a disabled little girl. I'll call the newspaper and the city and tell them, too."

"Oh, shut up."

And just like that, they quietly held each other until they fell asleep. Eventually, the light peeking in through the curtainless glass door turned from orange into deep blue. Right by the bedside was a cardboard box that rustled when Tsuneo's hand hit it.

"What in the world?" he muttered as he opened it to reveal something wrapped in a white bag.

"Those are my grandma's ashes," Josee mentioned amusedly. Her father had said he was going to come pick them up, but he still hadn't stopped by. Half the cardboard box was plastered with pictures of foreign cities.

Tsuneo didn't want to leave, so he stayed the night and was welcomed the next morning by wonderful early spring weather. He decided to take Josee outside for the first time in a few months. After calling as many friends as he could, he was eventually able to borrow someone's car that could fit both Josee and her wheelchair. Josee, however, was sulking.

"What's wrong?" Tsuneo asked her. "We don't have to go anywhere if you don't want to. We can stay inside today."

"Nuh-uh. I'm just in a bad mood right now 'cause I'm so happy. That's all."

Tsuneo laughed and kissed her. Just looking at her made him want to lock them both in the apartment and sleep with her again. The view of her slender, doll-like legs was strangely erotic, and between them was a quivering bottomless trap that held Tsuneo spellbound.

Josee ended up asking him to take her to the zoo. When she was living at the care facility, some of the volunteers took her to the zoo on a bus, but there was a time limit, so they only got to see the birds, monkeys, and elephants before having to leave. It was a big place that quickly tired out people with disabilities.

Josee said she wanted to see the tigers, so Tsuneo showed her to where the wild cats were kept. The zoo was surprisingly crowded for a weekday; maybe the first day of nice spring weather had drawn them all here. One look at the tiger, and Josee was unsurprisingly hooked. She watched in fascination as it tirelessly paced back and forth in its cage in a way unique to predators.

The tiger's deranged golden eyes full of silent, ferocious energy fixated on Josee, causing her to tremble in fear. However, her morbid curiosity was far stronger than any urge to look away.

The beast stopped right in front of Josee. She froze with terror to the point that she started struggling to breathe. The tiger then took one front limb, which looked strong enough to kill an elephant in a single swipe, and struck the concrete terrain in frustration before letting out a roar.

Its vivid golden and black fur glittered in the sunlight as it writhed, and its roar was so terrifying that Josee almost fainted.

"That thing's gonna give me nightmares...," she said, clinging to Tsuneo.

"Why'd you wanna see it if it scares you so much?"

"'Cause I wanted to see whatever scared me the most...once I met the love of my life. That way I could hold on to him like this," she explained. "I thought I'd go see a tiger as soon as I found that someone. And if I never found anybody, then I guess I'd just never see a real tiger in person. I couldn't let that bother me, though."

From high above, the island seemed hidden among a mass of greenery surrounded by ocean. The weather was hot and muggy, typical of southern Japan, and the lush trees were stubbornly verdant, making the island resemble a giant ball of moss.

There was an underwater aquarium here, which was why Josee had been asking Tsuneo to bring her for a visit. The island was part of an archipelago at the farthest point in Kyushu, so a day trip wasn't feasible. Therefore, Tsuneo decided to take some time off work to bring Josee here, since she adored zoos and aquariums so much.

A massive red bridge connected the island to the mainland. It looked like a long piece of yarn attached to the island. *Just like a yo-yo*, Josee thought. The expressway ran up through the mountains, occasionally obscuring the island and bridge from view until they reappeared even larger than before. The next thing they knew, Tsuneo and Josee had reached the bridge.

The bridge was dizzyingly high up and intimidating. It didn't help that the ocean below looked incredibly distant. Once they finally crossed it, Tsuneo and Josee continued through a parking lot full of sightseeing buses. Tsuneo followed the signs to a coastal road that snaked through a fourth of the island, until they eventually arrived at a beachside resort hotel.

"Hey, I called you guys earlier. Said I wanted a room on the first floor. Something wheelchair-friendly," Tsuneo told a hotel worker as he pulled the folded wheelchair out of the trunk of the car.

The young man in the black suit who came to greet them was making every effort not to look down at Josee's feet, to the point that Tsuneo actually started to feel bad for him.

Josee was wearing a long light-pink skirt along with a pink short-sleeved shirt. She was in a haughty mood with her chin held high, not even sparing a glance in the young man's direction, much less offering him a polite smile. The hotel employee eyed her as if she were a doll in an unopened box.

"We have a room for you on the second floor," he said. "The resort has an elevator, so you can use the banquet hall and cafeteria on the first floor whenever you like."

However, the elevator ended up being too small for the wheelchair to fit, so Tsuneo had to hoist Josee onto his back instead. The bellhop folded the wheelchair and carried it up to their room for them. A tour group of middle-aged women was making no effort not to stare at Josee, which got her really annoyed.

Tsuneo had told the hotel that they were on their honeymoon, so their room was decorated with flowers. Once the bellhop left…

"This is all your fault, Caretaker! You should've checked if the elevator was big enough to fit a wheelchair before you booked the room! Those old ladies were staring at me the entire time!" Josee howled with fury.

"Hey, Josee, forget about that for a sec and check out this view. Just look at that ocean."

Tsuneo opened the curtains and marveled at the sight. Outside the bay window was a panoramic vista of the sea, which put Josee in a slightly better mood. She climbed over the table and across the chairs, then gazed at the ocean in silence.

"There's really an aquarium down there?" she asked.

"Yep."

"Hurry up and let's go, then."

"Gimme a second to breathe, okay? I'm tired from driving all day."

"Then you don't have to come! I don't need you! I'll just ask the bellhop to take me."

Tsuneo heaved a deep sigh, then decided to take Josee straight to the aquarium. He still needed the bellhop's help, though. The aquarium was eight meters below ground, and the only way to get there was via the long concrete staircase. Tsuneo managed to carry Josee down the stairs and had the bellhop bring the wheelchair for them.

All of a sudden, they were surrounded by faint lights. Once Josee was back in her wheelchair, the bellhop departed the aquarium, leaving Josee and Tsuneo to themselves. The walls and ceiling were made of glass, and the seawater had a clear green tint to it. Rows of tiny cobalt fish swam through the swaying seaweed as vivid red fish passed them by.

Crawling along the sand at the bottom were eels, crabs, shrimp, and turtles. The only sounds were Tsuneo's footsteps and the creaking wheelchair; it must have been just the two of them there. A long silver and blue fish slowly came into view—a yellowtail.

Greater amberjack, black sea bream, and banded dogfish swam through the tank, brushing against the coral reef. Their eyes were dry, and each one looked slightly more human than the last.

"Wow. It was more than worth it coming all the way here. This is great," said Tsuneo, simply enjoying himself.

Josee, however, couldn't even speak. Down here, where you couldn't tell whether it was night or day, Josee felt as if she and Tsuneo were all alone at the bottom of the sea. She was entranced—borderline terrified—looping around the aquarium over and over again. Tsuneo eventually lost patience and scolded her, then had the lady at the ticket stand call for the bellhop before carrying Josee back up the staircase. By the time they got to the top, Tsuneo was already panting. They came face-to-face with the bright summer sunshine and the gift shop, and the salty sea air tickled their noses. The two of them decided to have some iced coffee at the nearby parlor before heading back up to the hotel, where they ordered room service.

When Josee woke up late into the night, the moonlight peeking through the opened curtains lit up the room like an underwater grotto in an aquarium.

Both Josee and Tsuneo were fish.

I must've died, Josee thought. *We both must've died.*

Tsuneo started living with Josee from then on. They were planning on getting married, but they never changed their family register, or announced a wedding, or even told Tsuneo's parents. Josee's grandmother's ashes remained in that same cardboard box, too.

And Josee was fine with this. She would take her time cooking and flavor the food just as Tsuneo liked. She'd leisurely wash his clothes and make sure that Tsuneo looked his absolute best. The two of them would carefully save their money so that they could go on a trip like this once a year.

We're both dead. Just a couple of bodies.

Dead bodies was what she meant.

Josee let out a sigh of deep satisfaction at their fishlike bodies. She didn't know if Tsuneo would leave her one day, but she was happy as long as he was by her side. That was enough. And in Josee's mind, happiness felt synonymous with death. Absolute happiness was death itself.

We're fish. Just a couple of bodies was her way of saying they were happy.

Josee laced her fingers through Tsuneo's, leaned into him, and pushed her beautifully slender yet limp doll-like legs closer before falling back into a peaceful slumber.

Men Hate Muffins

I finally got a call three days after arriving at the vacation house. Ren was practically glowing on the other end of the line. He seemed to love making a woman wait for him while he worked. He loved work so much it was as if he were born to do it. At forty-two years old, he was still single and working as the CEO of an apparel company.

"What's up, Mimi?"

"I don't know. You tell me."

I was about to explode with rage until I heard Ren's voice, and it annoyed me that there was even a hint of joy in mine.

"I went through a lot of trouble to take time off from work, you know. And you're not even here. What am I? Your maid? Want me to clean the place before I leave?"

"Oh, don't be like that. I took time off, too, but I suddenly got—"

"Fine, it's fine. Just tell me when you're going to get here. I've already wasted three days of my week off. I'm fine with packing my stuff and leaving if you're gonna take any longer. I didn't think you could do any worse than when I was in Hawaii, but here we are."

"Wait, Mimi. Please. I'll be there as soon as I can, just not tonight. I've still gotta meet someone later for dinner, and it's probably gonna be a long evening. But tomorrow—"

"So you're saying you'll be here tomorrow?"

"I don't know, but just wait for me, okay? Please."

"Oh, come on…"

Ren Torii was a child. That is, he acted like a kid who complained if an adult confiscated his candy, even if he wasn't actually in the mood for candy at that moment.

Hey, wait! I was gonna eat that! Give it back!

He'd throw a tantrum, but if he did get his candy back, he'd just hold onto it without eating it.

"I'll be there, I'll be there," he said in an attempt to reassure me. *"Besides, you can have a nice time alone at the house, too. Have the chef at Uomasa cook something for you."*

"Oh, a 'nice time'? I've got motorcycle gangs revving their engines outside my window every night. Last year was nothing like this."

"Ah. Huh."

"It's awful. Hurry up and get over here."

"I want to, Mimi, especially after hearing your voice. I want to see you right now," he insisted. *"Mimi."*

"What?"

"I love you. Really, I do."

"How about you stop wasting time talking and get over here instead? It's your loss if a good catch like me gets tired of waiting for you."

"Gonna leave me for one of those bikers?"

"Maybe I will. I've always preferred young bad boys over middle-aged workaholics."

"Damn, you got me." Ren said that only when he was happy. *"I wish I had two bodies: one for work and one for you."*

He sounded satisfied with that remark.

"Hmph. That'd just water you down, make you even blander than you already are."

"Man, I'd do anything to see you tonight. But I've got dinner plans, then tomorrow I'm meeting a client for golf…"

"So cancel. It's just this one time. They couldn't possibly feel more neglected than I've felt the past three days."

Ren usually ate both lunch and dinner at work, so I knew what I was talking about.

"I can't cancel. You know that. Anyway, I'll make sure to be there as soon as I'm done."

Right as he was about to hang up…

"Oh, what do they have at Uomasa these days?"

"Yesterday was sardines. They said they'd make some into a *tataki* for me."

"Did you have any?"

"I'm not gonna ask them to do all that work just for one person."

"Fine, fine. Anyway, this is making me even more excited to see you. I'll be there soon, so don't go cheating on me, okay?"

"Oh, I totally will!"

Ren laughed as if that was the funniest thing he'd heard all day.

"Is the bath working?"

"Yeah. Why?"

"Wash up before I get there, okay? Wink, wink."

"Screw you, asshole."

"I can send Shimon if you're really bored."

"I'd rather him than you anyway. Just don't blame me for whatever happens."

"Oh, come on. Don't be like that. You know I can't let you hang out with him. The guy's in love with you."

"He's still a kid."

"Kids these days can be scary."

"It's your fault he turned out this way."

"Nah. I saw you egging him on, Mimi."

Now I was the one laughing.

Shimon was Ren's nephew who worked part-time at Ren's company while attending college. I'd gone out to eat with the two of them several times in the past.

Shimon was a really friendly guy, and he seemed to be interested in me, so Ren and I would joke about him whenever we were flirting like this. I had absolutely no interest in kids his age—he just made for the perfect punch line.

Ren hung up in a very good mood. I couldn't stop thinking about his delightful, expressive face. He wasn't handsome. In fact, he was short and a bit chubby, but I found him charming and adorable. I know it's a little strange that a thirty-one-year-old woman like me—eleven years Ren's junior—landed a man in his forties and considered him to be the most lovable thing in the world, but hey.

I found his steamy, hot-blooded body attractive as well. Whenever he held me, I felt like I'd just been rescued by a lifeguard who was wrapping my waterlogged body in a warm blanket. It was like being given hot soup as my teeth chattered from fear and the cold, my body slowly warming from the inside out.

Sex with Ren was like being rescued, too. I loved every minute of it; he was very gentle.

I didn't have much experience with men, but based on the few encounters I did have, I got the sense that age had nothing to do with being good at sex. Some old folks sucked at it, some young folks had a knack for it, plus there was always the question of how creative or sensitive a person was in bed. No way men who were stupid or thoughtless would be any good in the sack.

As much as Ren enjoyed sex, he also enjoyed his job. A little too much, even, and that was where I had a problem. After I graduated from design school and got hired within the industry, I started writing occasional articles for fashion magazines before quitting my job and moving to Tokyo. I liked design, so I ended up becoming an illustrator who wrote on the side. Before long, work kept me constantly busy to the point that I was able to support myself.

Tokyo was also where I met Ren Torii, during a magazine interview. We got along really well, so we went out for drinks after work. The following day, I got a voicemail while I was still asleep in bed.

"I'm heading back to Osaka today, so I thought I'd call you to say goodbye."

It was Ren, sounding very giddy.

"I had a lot of fun last night. Thanks for that. Gimme a ring if you're ever in Osaka. We'll go out for some drinks."

He'd married young but got a divorce after his daughter was born, and he ended up single. I don't know exactly what happened; maybe his wife left him because he was so obsessed with his work. Regardless, Ren's a talkative, friendly guy, so he must've won ladies over rather easily. Japanese men have never been known for being good talkers, so he probably stood out for being so smooth.

"I love plucky, frank ladies like you. I'm not into playing mind games. My company makes women's clothing that's feminine and elegant, but personally, I prefer tomboys. Especially a woman who can rock a leather jacket."

It was the middle of winter when I met him again in Osaka, and I wore a black leather jacket with dark-brown corduroy pants. There was absolutely nothing sexy about that outfit, but Ren Torii's eyes filled with desire the moment he saw me, and his plump lips loosened amorously. He was captivated the moment he laid eyes on me, completely defenseless.

That defenselessness was what drew me in, and what I mean by that is I liked how he didn't get defensive when I poked fun at him. People these days don't like being teased. The thought alone puts them on edge. Ren, however, didn't seem to mind. He let me get close enough to make a fool of him. That was why I fell in love with the man. That, and this rescuer sex appeal he had, which I naturally picked up on. I almost immediately found myself thinking, *I wouldn't mind sleeping with this guy.*

Half a year went by before our relationship developed enough for that to happen, though. Ren said he wouldn't mind taking things to the next level if I wanted to get married, but we only occasionally met up in Tokyo and Osaka for the three years that followed.

When he said I could have a nice time alone at this house, he meant it. Ren loved the beach and had built a semi-fancy hilltop vacation home on the outskirts of a remote fishing village in Okayama Prefecture. I've never been to the Mediterranean coast, but this place reminded me of a European farmhouse with an ocean view. He'd apparently hired an architect from Osaka to design it, and the tiles in the front yard came from a local company. The spacious entranceway had cool stone flooring.

The grassy, tree-lined backyard boasted a view of the ocean, which always struck me as crowded from the constant stream of boats going between the islands of the Setouchi archipelago. The vacation house was surrounded by a stone fence and hedges that had become so overgrown through the years that they were now climbing up the house, making it look more like a fairy-tale castle. A gardener from a neighboring village would stop by a few times a year to trim the hedges.

There was also a local fishmonger called Uomasa that would deliver fish straight to your house, even cook something up and bring it over. Even on a harbor, there were a lot of complicated rules and regulations within the fishing industry, like how there were some things you weren't allowed to catch. Fishermen patronized Uomasa as well.

In the vacation house's white-tiled front yard was a pink-tinted marble statue of a nymph and a fountain to go along with it. Every window had vermilion shutters, and wherever there wasn't grass, there was a paving stone instead. Even the white front door's handle had an elaborate design. There were two bedrooms, two bathrooms, a dining room, a kitchen, and a living room. Both bedrooms were on the second floor in order to have that view of the sea.

It got hot during the summertime, but the fragrant ocean air was lovely. A four-to-five-hundred-meter walk up the beach brought you to a resort hotel and a guesthouse. Those in the know recognized this spot as having the best view of the Seto Inland Sea.

Having a vacation home with a seaside view was Ren's dream. The house was basically the other woman in his life; he didn't actually have to visit it, since he was happy enough merely knowing it existed. Granted, he'd certainly disagree with that sentiment: *No way. Of course I want to go to my vacation house, but I'm so busy.*

Nevertheless, we spent three whole days here together last year. After taking a morning shower, we would walk across the dew-covered grass while enjoying our hot coffee and garlic toast. I became very fond of this vacation home.

The path at the bottom of the stone staircase in the backyard led straight through a thicket to the shore. The beach was far from the area the fishing boats used, so the water wasn't polluted with oil. Unfortunately, however, it wasn't as blue or as clear as the beaches in the South Pacific Ocean. Here, the water was reddish-brown, and yet people still swam in it, us included.

Ren and I had sashimi from Uomasa for lunch one day, and I used the leftover fish parts to make miso soup. That evening, we watered the lawn and took a bath together, but every minute in between, he was on the phone with someone from his office.

We went to a hotel for dinner that night, and I asked him over a Campari and soda, "Why did you and your wife split up?"

This was one way I liked to tease him.

"It was a deep-seated grudge," he'd answered with a grin.

"A grudge?"

"My wife didn't work like you do, Mimi. I mean, there's nothing wrong with staying home just takin' it easy and enjoying yourself. But it was almost like that wasn't good enough for her. She'd complain day in and day out until eventually, she got resentful. It's hard being with someone who holds grudges. It slowly became unbearable."

The phrase *deep-seated grudge* blew me away. It made me like him even more. *I want us to spend our lives together. Doesn't matter if we get married or not*, I thought, and Ren agreed.

"Yeah, exactly. Getting married means becoming a family...but becoming a family isn't so much sexy as it is lewd," he said.

"I'm fine with sexy."

"Right? Bring it on, I say. Glad we're on the same page."

And being on that same page made him even hotter. A hot rescuer. I loved the weight of Ren's body, its heft syrupy, like honey covering every inch of my body. I loved throwing open the bedroom window and listening to the night breeze whistling through the shutters as I lay wrapped in Ren, my rescue blanket, after being saved from getting stranded at sea.

Once the evening wind began blowing, I took a shower, peeked inside the fridge, and made frozen steak for dinner. The house had a television—Ren wanted to know what was going on in the world even when he was staying here, so he would watch TV and call people up—but I never turned it on when I was by myself.

After dinner, I locked up for the night and began reading the book I brought with me, *The Notebook of Black Magic* by Tatsuhiko Shibusawa. It was muggy out. I knew Ren wasn't coming tonight, either, so I was bored.

At around eight o'clock, I suddenly started hearing motorcycles getting closer, along with the shouts of men as they revved their roaring engines. It startled me so much that I felt my heart leap in my chest.

They passed the house, then came back from the opposite direction and circled around before fading into the distance again. That was when I realized they were racing up the back street behind the house and circling the hill.

I felt helpless, surrounded. Who knew what they'd do to me if they found out a woman was here alone? I started running around the house in my bare feet, closing each and every shutter I could find. How ridiculous, being this worked up when I was alone on vacation. I resented Ren for it.

Speaking of resentment, we'd promised to go to Hawaii together a short while back, but minutes before the plane was about to depart, Ren still hadn't shown up. I cried, begging the flight attendant to wait for him, and just when I thought it was too late, Ren came sprinting over, covered in sweat and without a single suitcase. We got onto the plane as soon as the door closed, and moments later, it started preparing for takeoff.

Ren fell asleep basically the instant he sat down and spent most of our time in Hawaii asleep as well. It didn't take long for our bad moods to worsen until we clashed.

"I've had enough of this! You're always busy! Busy, busy, busy, busy, busy, busy! I'm sick of hearing how busy you are!" I'd shouted in tears after we got into a fight.

"Aw, don't be like that, Mimi. It's only 'cause you're here with me that I'm able to get all relaxed like this…"

Ren had tried comforting me at first, but he started trailing off and fell back asleep. In the end, it was as if we'd gone to Hawaii for the sole purpose of sleeping.

Just remembering that made me resent him. Did he honestly think I was going to wait here for him forever? How insulting. I was even annoyed that he called me. I didn't want to talk to him if he wasn't going to come here. I refused.

If he was only going to call me to say he couldn't make it, then I wish he'd never promised he'd be here in the first place. Why even make these plans if he couldn't keep them?

The motorcycle noises returned, and it sounded as if the front yard's iron lattice gate had been opened (the latch could be removed from the outside as well). I suddenly got nervous and turned out the lights. I didn't want these people to know anyone was here.

I saw several sharp beams of light peeking through the shutters and began hearing strange sounds. I was terrified. When I cautiously peeked through the front door window, I caught the words *Demon Coalition* written on the closest man's helmet. There were seven to eight motorcycles and bikers all crowded around the yard, cheering and revving their engines until they finally left.

I searched for the padlock, locked the iron gate, then lay down in the bedroom. I wasn't used to such frightening experiences, so I was kind of in shock. The bikers had strong accents, something I was normally fond of, but in that moment, I felt nothing but fear.

The next morning, I figured maybe they weren't such bad guys, after all. They were probably just really into motorcycles. Maybe reading *The Notebook of Black Magic* made my imagination run wild.

However, the yard had tire marks in it, and some of the tiles were cracked. It looked like they'd been riding in circles all over the lawn; even one of the wooden chairs was knocked over.

I called Ren's place. He was living alone in a midtown apartment near his office. I caught him right before he left for work.

"Geez, you poor thing. That does sound terrifying," he agreed. If he really felt that way, he would've said he'd come right over, which he didn't.

"I'm going home. Back to Tokyo," I told him.

"Hold on. Why are you leaving already? Wait for me. I'll be there soon," he pleaded.

"No way. I'm scared."

"All right, then how about I send Shimon over to protect you? He can be your bodyguard. Just stay put, okay?"

I thought he was teasing me.

The weather was nice that day, so I decided to tend to the garden, clean the house, take a nap, and do some window shopping at Uomasa. They were selling sea bream today. I went with sardines again since I wasn't planning on waiting up for Ren. There was no telling when he'd be here. The sardines were freshly caught, with glittering silver scales, so I bought a whole bunch. I also ended up baking some simple muffins just in case Shimon really did come tomorrow. I figured muffins would be perfect for a hungry young man who was still growing. The sun was beginning to set, so I decided to go take a dip in the hotel pool after that.

Being alone in such a luxurious vacation home made me feel out of sorts, as if I were aimlessly floating through the air. I didn't own the place, nor was it my husband's… Ren and I weren't going to get married, and what we had was too bland to call ourselves lovers… Even if he did show up, he'd just be relieved to see me, and that would be it.

Ren badmouthed his ex-wife a lot, but maybe any woman would grow resentful being with a man like him.

The hotel was completely booked. I didn't see anyone I knew at the pool, so I was able to relax and swim to my heart's content. It was crowded; there seemed to be a lot of girls staying at the nearby guesthouse.

I was wearing a blue terrycloth robe over my swimsuit as I walked back to the house from the pool. My hair was still dripping wet, but the hotel showers were packed, so I didn't have much of a choice. I had a straw hat pushed down the back of my head as well as dark-tinted sunglasses. When I finally stepped into the yard, I found a young man standing in front of the pink marble nymph statue. It was Shimon.

It looked like he'd been strolling through the yard for a bit until he spotted me.

"Hey," he said with a smile.

He was so much tanner and taller that I almost didn't recognize him. Shimon was becoming more of a man every time I saw him. He said he took a bus straight from the bullet train and had just arrived here a few moments ago. Shimon was very friendly and talkative like Ren, and he said whatever what was on his mind, which seemed to be a family quirk.

He grinned despite himself. "I'm so glad to be here. I was really looking forward to seeing you, Ms. Mimi. I'll be leaving when my uncle arrives, though. Said he'd be here tomorrow."

"I doubt that. He'll probably call tomorrow and tell me that something suddenly came up."

I then took Shimon to the backyard.

"The breeze is much nicer back here," I boasted as if I owned this vacation house.

I took a shower after that. I wasn't as much of an open book as Shimon, so although I didn't look happy, I was honestly really glad to see him. Chatting with someone who said he'd been looking forward to seeing me was way more fun than talking with my boyfriend, who probably wasn't even going to show up.

My pure-white dress fluttered in the wind as I put on my white sandals and stepped outside, two Camparis with soda in hand. The evening sun had begun painting the sky. I wouldn't call it beautiful, though—more like grim. After taking a seat in the lawn chairs out back, we watched the ocean until the shadows of the islands in the distance got noticeably darker. The sky, however, was rather bright, and I could still see clearly in front of me. Clamorous crows gathered in the thickets in the woods to my right, where there was a shrine at the cape.

Gazing at the ocean from the shrine gate felt kind of like I was observing an archipelago from some ancient Greek ruins. Ren and I enjoyed the view, so we often went on walks there.

"When did you get here?" Shimon asked before taking a sip of the drink I'd made him.

"Three days ago."

"That long already?"

He probably hadn't put much thought into that comment, but I was worried he might think I was waiting here longingly for Ren, desperately yearning for his arrival. It almost sounded like Shimon was making fun of me.

"I haven't been waiting for him. Do I look like a woman who would just wait around helplessly without her man?"

"No, I just wished I'd known sooner. Then I could've been here three days ago." Shimon's gaze shifted. "Plus, I heard something about a biker gang?"

"They called themselves the Demon Coalition. How stupid is that? But it was really scary, since I was alone. It didn't help that I was reading this book. I thought the bikers were holding a Black Mass or something."

I showed him the book by Tatsuhiko Shibusawa, took a hit of my bitter drink, and read one of the poems aloud.

"'My gray gloves permanently soak in life's divine liquid. With my furnace, I surrendered myself to alchemy like Hermes at the break of dawn in severe winters.

"'In the evenings of summer, I concealed demons into my daggers like the alchemist Paracelsus, angering the scholars in the streets.'

"...There actually was an alchemist named Paracelsus, by the way."

Shimon quietly watched me the entire time I recited the passage. I flipped to this page and read the part about Paracelsus so often that the book would naturally open to this passage whenever I picked it up. I wondered why he was staring at me, when all of a sudden...

"Found a gray hair," he said while he reached out to touch my bangs.

Maybe I was going gray early, but my short hair made it stick out like a sore thumb. I knocked his hand away.

"I like finding my gray hairs on my own. I don't like it when other people stare at them."

"I just thought I could pluck it out for you."

"Don't."

"Can I touch your hair?"

"It's still wet."

"It's half-dry."

I kind of felt like Shimon—this kid—was patronizing me, but he didn't appear to mean any harm. He combed his fingers through my hair.

"Now go hop in the shower," I told him. "I'll make some food."

I ended up making minced sardines on rice, even though that was what Ren wanted to eat. At first, Shimon said he didn't like fish and had never eaten sardines before—just like a kid his age would—but he cleaned his huge bowl, not leaving a single grain of rice.

I grated garlic and ginger, then placed heaps of spring onion and grated radish with chili on top. The fresh, raw sardines were so good that you could eat them all day and never get sick of them. I also salted a few sardines and broiled them, which complemented the sardine tempura I made. I'd been soaking some globeflowers I picked from the garden yesterday in water, which I boiled with soy sauce and mixed with rice. We drank only a little beer but stuffed our faces with the food.

"Wonder if those bikers are gonna come back today," Shimon said.

"You better not pull anything risky."

"I was just planning on holding you till they left, Mimi."

He dropped the *Ms.* and was just calling me Mimi now. There was no beating this family, was there? They ate what they wanted to eat, did what they felt like doing, said whatever was on their minds.

"Do you like me?" I asked Shimon.

"Yeah, I do. But you like the old man, don't you?"

"Eh, I guess. I haven't gotten sick of him yet, at the very least. What, you hate him or something?"

"Nah, I don't hate him. Sometimes, I even like him better than my folks. Anyway, enough about my family... But really, though, I wonder why he's still not here when you've been waiting for him this long."

"He likes making people wait. Loves being irritated at work while fantasizing about leaving at any moment."

"Makes no sense. Sounds like a midlife crisis."

We washed the dishes together while telling each other our likes and dislikes. I told him I liked figs, that one card game Concentration, strawberry milk, dogs, fireworks, and gossip. And of course, I couldn't *not* mention Marquise de Merteuil in *Les Liaisons dangereuses.* Shimon didn't like confined spaces, the *Asahi Shimbun*, girls who pretended to be cute, girls who got smashed every night, and abalone liver.

"Find a job yet?" I suddenly asked.

"Aw, c'mon, don't start. That's another thing I don't like: smug old ladies. Besides, I know you don't really care."

"Nope. I'd rather know if you've been with any women yet."

"You gotta be kidding me…," Shimon said with a laugh.

He told me he'd lost his virginity, and his friend accidentally brought it up in front of his mother, who immediately burst into tears from the shock. She'd apparently spent the entire next day in bed.

"I dunno why she made such a big deal about it. She should've just pretended she didn't hear anything," he said.

I suddenly remembered my conversation with Ren about how becoming a family was lewd, but I didn't bring it up. Obviously, I wasn't shocked or even disgusted that Shimon wasn't a virgin. After all, I wasn't his mother. If anything, I was more disgusted by how *she* had reacted.

Shimon and I spread a deck of cards on the table and started playing Concentration while drinking some refreshing whiskey soda. I'd developed my own trick to memorizing cards, so I started the game feeling pretty confident. I ended up finding one matching set after another, netting me most of the deck. I made sure to close the window so the breeze wouldn't blow the cards off the table, and thankfully, it wasn't that hot out. Closing the window blocked out most outside noise, although I probably wouldn't have noticed anyway, since I was so focused on the game.

"You hear something?" Shimon asked, tapping my hand. Now that he mentioned it, I could hear the roaring of engines in the distance.

"It's them," I said.

Shimon opened the window. A row of headlights shone through the hedges by the gate, so he went outside. I asked him if he was sure about this, but he didn't answer.

"Evening," he called as he leaned against the iron gate. The men on the other side of the gate seemed to be saying something back.

I turned on the TV, figuring it was better to make it look like there were a few more people inside just in case.

"You can't pass through here, sorry. Too many bushes. I'd appreciate it if you didn't cut through the yard," Shimon told them.

I have no idea what the bikers said back, but I heard their motorcycles begin heading down the street. I thought they were going to circle the house like they did last night, but they simply went down the hill before fading into the distance.

They were apparently a fickle bunch. When Shimon asked them not to drive through the yard, they just made fun of his accent, then left. He said they were all guys in their late teens.

He seemed rather laid-back about the whole thing, but I was nervous. I was honestly sweating bullets, worried something was going to happen to him. I'd never worry this much if it were Ren, but those bikers were around Shimon's age, and I was concerned they'd feel like he was taunting them. Apparently, I got all worked up for nothing.

After Shimon turned off the lights at the front door and came back inside, I immediately threw my arms around his waist and hugged him tight.

"Oh, thank goodness! I was so scared."

"I was only able to all say that 'cause I'm drunk. I dunno what I'd do if I was sober." Shimon wrapped his arms around my shoulders. "And I dunno what I'm doing right now, either, 'cause I'm drunk," he mumbled as he tried to kiss me, but I managed to slip away.

"Oh—Shimon, I made muffins. Want any?"

I returned with a basket of raisin muffins I'd baked from flour, baking powder, eggs, milk, and some vegetable oil. They looked really tasty for how simple the recipe was.

"Nah, I hate anything sweet like that," Shimon answered.

Come to think of it, Ren loved my cooking but hated sweets as well.

Shimon and I slept in separate bedrooms that night. He must have been exhausted, because he fell asleep instantly. His room was completely silent.

It rained the next day. I was going to take Shimon to the hotel pool, but unfortunately, those plans fell through.

"Bet the old man would play golf even in the rain. I wonder if he'll be here today." He seemed really curious if Ren was coming or not.

Then he gazed vacantly out the window. "Man, I drank way too much last night."

"You did?"

"I went downstairs in the middle of the night and had some booze."

"Oh my."

"It started pouring then, so I watched the rain as I drank. Did a bit of thinking. I was debating whether I should wake you up to have someone to talk to."

I was making omelets for breakfast.

"Would've rather slept with you than talk, though," he continued. "But I didn't, 'cause that's what the old man was expecting me to do. I didn't want to feel like a pawn in his game."

That sounded accurate to me. Ren was probably worried that Shimon and I would do something, and that frustration caused him to enjoy work even more. He'd get busier and busier with work until that became his sole focus. Maybe he would wonder how I felt, and that energized him, making it even less likely for him to come here. Maybe I was merely a pawn Ren used to get enthusiastic about his job.

Shimon's face was swollen black and blue, perhaps due to all the drinking and the weather.

The front yard's pink marble nymph statue glistened in the rain, and the white tiling reflected the greenery. Only the sound of raindrops filled the air.

Suddenly, I said, "Shimon, want to get out of here? I'm not gonna wait for him anymore."

"Okay."

"Let's take a trip somewhere, just the two of us."

"Sure."

We stood by the rain-drenched window, my arms wrapped tightly around his waist. His hair and lips were soft.

There wasn't any bread to go with the omelets. I briefly thought we could have the muffins instead, but that was when I realized that I didn't really like muffins that much, either. I'd only made them to satisfy my own ego, thinking they'd make me look good.

I hadn't brought much with me: just makeup, some clothes, and that book by Tatsuhiko Shibusawa. Oh, and now I was leaving with something even bigger: Shimon.

I retired from the vacation house with its beautiful view of the ocean. The boats passed one another through the foggy sea and unrelenting rain.

Until It Snows

It was a rather gloomy house. The gate had already halfway fallen apart and was very narrow due to the overgrown vegetation. The stepping stones were covered in moss, making the entranceway even gloomier and darker. There was no nameplate.

The woman who came out of the house was around forty years old and dressed in typical housewife attire: a sweater, skirt, and white socks.

Iwako asked her for Oba.

"Come in," said the woman. "He's waiting for ya."

She spoke casually and made no attempt at faking a smile, but her expression was friendly. She seemed very accustomed to welcoming and entertaining guests.

The house was bitterly cold and dank. It must have been quite old. The hallway was dim, and the rooms with sliding doors appeared to be empty. The hallway floor was hair-raisingly chilly.

The woman suddenly took a left at the end of the hallway.

"Here we are…" She got on her knees and called out to the person in the room, "Your guest has arrived."

She carefully opened the darkened sliding door with both hands.

Oba was sitting next to the window. After the woman left, Iwako took off her coat and said, "Sorry I'm late... Were you waiting long?"

Iwako always spoke quietly. People often told her so at the fabric shop where she worked in Azuchimachi, Osaka. Nevertheless, her voice was perfectly audible, so nobody found it particularly bothersome. Her already quiet voice became even quieter when she spoke to Oba.

"No, not at all. Don't worry about it," he calmly assured her, although Iwako still thought he'd probably been waiting a while.

"It's quite dark in here..."

"Yeah, but they feed you well. This is my second time, so trust me. I'll make sure you're satisfied."

Oba was a fifty-one-year-old man, but his voice was strong and full of life. Maybe it was from all the Noh chanting he did. Iwako was invited to a Noh meetup once before, but...

"Please. Anything but that," she'd declined. Oba had apparently been learning tea ceremony with his wife, but Iwako didn't do that, either.

"Sorry I'm so uncultured," she once told him.

"Liking tea ceremony doesn't make you cultured. Truly refined women like to have fun—like you," Oba joked. "In fact, it's not just women. Having the leeway to take the time to enjoy yourself is what makes anyone refined."

"Well, I'm already forty-six. I'm sure all people are like this when they're this old."

"Not at all. You would think that, but it's actually quite unusual. If you go to the red-light district, it becomes all about money, and amateurs are bound by the shackles of convention..."

"Ha-ha-ha."

"So no, Iwako, you're one in a million. There's no one else like you."

Iwako had been spending time with Oba for the past year, but her heart still hadn't stopped racing whenever she was around him. Every time she saw him, she would be too shy to meet his eyes for the first few minutes. Whenever Oba looked at her fondly, she'd stare at the ground as tears began to well in her eyes. It was happiness mixed with bashfulness. She got so excited that she could hardly breathe and so nervous that she would start feeling dizzy. Iwako would even start regretting coming over to see him. That's how much of a mess she became around him. Her skin would slowly flush crimson as well.

Iwako looked slender because she knew how to dress and carry herself, yet she was actually a heavy woman. Her smooth, luscious skin, white as porcelain, glowed coyly whenever she was around Oba.

Oba pulled her closer.

"…But what about that woman?" Iwako whispered.

"Don't worry about her. She's very slow. Everything here is done in slow motion," he replied with a laugh. "Anyway, I need to warm you up before you get colder."

There was a single small portable heater in the room and nothing else. It was a very traditional house in that way.

Oba's lean, muscular body didn't have an ounce of fat on it. He was quite tall and brawny for a man his age. "I always used to be bigger than the others, but kids nowadays are all really tall," he once told Iwako.

How does he always make me feel this way? Iwako wondered in admiration as she leaned into Oba's tight embrace. The way he held her and the soft lips that fell upon her like warm snow were perfect. She fit perfectly, and that didn't just mean physically. Oba seemed to fit into the framework of her life like a missing puzzle piece. His body was hard, but his arms, tongue, and lips always felt so soft to her. It didn't feel like the body of a man—more like the steaming warmth of life. Iwako thought of his body as a sigh of satisfaction gently wrapping around her.

No other man had ever made her feel this way. Before she met Oba, she was with a thirty-eight or thirty-nine-year-old named Kuno.

Iwako had been doing accounting work for her fabric shop for over a decade. Around thirty to forty people worked there, and while the pay wasn't great, it was a very homey establishment. Everyone thought that Iwako, who looked very plain and reserved, was just a bland middle-aged woman. Even her older sister probably thought she was this gloomy spinster who had lost her chance of ever getting married.

And yet Iwako had this innate quality that only certain highly skilled men could somehow sense. That was how the playboy named Kuno came into her life.

Iwako was fastidious about dating these men who noticed this quality of hers and approached her—and no one else. She had zero interest in ever getting married; simply fooling around with men was very fulfilling.

I want to keep dating until I'm seventy or eighty…

Iwako was happy to pursue romantic endeavors even in old age. Men were something of a hobby of hers.

"I knew it… You're exactly how I imagined you'd be," Kuno whispered with deep satisfaction after the first time they'd slept together.

"Oh? And what do you mean by that?"

"Your skin. The first time we met, I thought your skin was so beautiful. Plus, there's the sounds you make."

"Sounds?"

"Yeah, the way you moan is so dirty."

"…Nobody's ever told me that before."

"That's 'cause they're a bunch of naive fools. You gotta be smart to pick up on how you sound when you moan."

"I wasn't trying to sound dirty…"

"It's a good thing. Your voice really makes the imagination run wild… You're not like other women. Something about you really stirs a man's carnal desires. All men have filthy minds deep down…"

"I've never been especially popular, though…"

"Psh, don't lie to me. You're too much of a freak in bed for me to believe that. Your kinkiness has flavor, like it's been simmering in a pot for a long time."

Kuno was a genuine idiot, but Iwako kind of liked that he could smell the freak on her and how he used the phrase *carnal desires*. Nonetheless, he was a player and quite shallow, so Iwako almost instantly got bored with him. He lacked flavor. She wanted to tell him to come back after he simmered in the pot a little longer.

"Some people can't see the forest for the trees," as the saying goes. Too much fooling around would become a drag and eventually cause Iwako to lose sight of her womanly desires—although perhaps that was simply the natural way of things (something that became clear to her when she compared other men with Oba).

Talking to Kuno had bored Iwako out of her skull. He didn't have a single good trait outside of the sack; he was just a fidgety guy who worked at a small print and copy shop in town.

Kuno would fidget and talk about what was happening on the inside at some religious organization—all secondhand info, too. His mother and wife had joined this group, and Kuno ended up eventually joining as well to get more work. He constantly complained about the leader, and Iwako quickly lost interest in Kuno, who probably thought he was doing her a favor by sleeping with her.

Ugh, I can't deal with this…

Iwako, meanwhile, had already mentally checked out of their affair and soon ended things. Kuno was vaguely handsome with his wire-framed glasses and had sort of a bad-boy appeal, which he seemed aware of. Iwako liked that about him.

Nevertheless, no man's charms were any match for Oba's. Iwako was currently infatuated with him, head over heels. Oba worked for a lumber company in Kyoto, and Iwako used to travel to Kyoto from time to time to learn flower arrangement. That was where she met him, at a flower arrangement workshop. He had been with his wife that day.

"She dragged me here," he said.

Oba's wife wore glasses, and her cheeks were plump and beautifully fair. They seemed to have a loving marriage. This workshop was in Kyoto, a major city, so there were plenty of male attendees, young and old alike. Iwako kept going to Kyoto at her teacher's insistence, but the workshop started getting in the way of her job, so she ended up dropping out. Iwako was never planning on teaching flower arrangement, nor was she interested in using a flower arranging diploma as a tool for marriage. She was only learning it for her own enjoyment, which was why she was free to start and quit whenever she wanted.

"You're not coming by anymore? It's going to be lonely without you," said Oba. They'd exchanged pleasantries over the past year that Iwako had been attending the workshop: *Good evening. Sure is hot today. Chilly out there, isn't it?*

That was the extent of their relationship, until...

"I hope I get to see you again," Oba said tenderly to Iwako and immediately took her hands in his.

It was cold that day, but Iwako wasn't wearing gloves. She thought his hands were extremely warm. His large, manly fingers wrapped around hers; it was the first time Iwako had ever experienced such a thing. No one had ever held her hands in theirs like this, even the men she slept with.

He's so soft and gentle, she thought. Oba clung to her like some otherworldly mollusk. *He's perfect. The perfect fit.*

Nevertheless, Iwako still didn't consider having a relationship with him at that time. After a year went by, she suddenly got a call from Oba saying that he was in Osaka. He apparently had some business to take care of in Yokobori, so they met in southern Osaka. That night was when it all began. They started meeting up once a month or three times every two months after that but never spent the night together. This went on for a year and a half. There's the storied cliché that "every day felt like a dream," but that was precisely how Iwako felt.

Her public life as "the clerk from Yamatake Fabrics" involved years and years of going to the bank, calculating bills, and bookkeeping. There was another seasoned accountant in the department who was related to the CEO, so Iwako didn't have any big responsibilities. She would even make tea for her coworkers and clean the shop. Reserved though she was, Iwako came across as friendly, so customers seemed to like her and consider her a nice lady.

Iwako always wore her hair the same way, used the same old bag, ate lunch that she made herself, and took the subway to and from work. She lived in a cheap, privately managed apartment in Sagisu and always bought one lottery ticket at a time, which the convenience store staff knew she put in her wallet. Iwako never seemed bothered by working overtime and would enjoy her favorite kitsune udon that the company bought for everyone, slurping up every last drop of broth. Once she was finished eating, she would collect everyone's bowls and wash them in the breakroom; she was very helpful in every sense of the word. The fabric shop sometimes hired young women who would normally end up getting married or finding a different job, making Iwako the only permanent presence—a very soothing one to both employees and customers alike.

So when the bank teller called for the clerk from Yamatake Fabrics and Iwako responded, nobody was able to tell how rich her life was, that every day felt like a dream to her.

Whenever Iwako thought about making love with Oba (she preferred the term *make love* to *sex* like people called it nowadays
because it seemed more accurate to their relationship), she felt as if
she were drowning in a sea of melancholic joy. She became acutely
aware of her womb, like how a person can feel the path a drink of
cold water takes as it slides through their body. Just like how Iwako
got her first period early, she started menopause early, or at least
she'd forgotten when she'd last had her period beginning the year
prior. And forgetting was the perfect thing for her. She'd even
started forgetting that she used to menstruate at all.

Iwako secretly believed this was the best part of her life, so she
didn't get sentimental about menopause. In fact, she likely didn't
care one bit about having a uterus. Iwako was aware of her womb
not as a physical object, but as female life itself.

It was the core to a woman's life and proof of her being.

Every time she recalled the excitement that making love with
Oba brought her, it felt as if a powerful, warm liquid drug was quietly passing through her body. She had no idea if they were going to
break up, but the mere thought of having met such a wonderful
man was enough to satisfy her. Of course, Iwako had no desire of
ever marrying Oba, and she liked that he similarly had no interest
in marriage. His relationship with his wife was going well, and he
had balance in his life, which Iwako liked, too. She cared about him
being married as much as she cared about people at the bank calling
her the clerk from Yamatake Fabrics for the past decade or so. It
didn't matter to her. It was simply another part of her day, like trans-
ferring and depositing money.

"Can I open a window?" Iwako asked quietly.

Just like a kiss that could melt ice, Iwako had opened herself up
to Oba but still felt shy at first whenever they met, as if she'd never
done any of this before.

"There's never any 'to be continued' with you. It always comes to an end, then the next time I see you, it's a fresh start," Oba had once told her.

Iwako herself wondered why she was like this, yet she nonetheless continued to struggle with the unbearable shyness that always came with seeing him.

"It's cold," Oba replied, but he still opened the paper sliding window for her.

Looming behind the cedar and cypress trees was Arashiyama. The sky was gray, and the trees changing color here and there on the dreary, dark-green mountain surface looked like the stripes of a tiger.

"We came to the coldest place in Kyoto at the coldest time of the year," Oba said with a chuckle, but Iwako didn't mind the chill. She remembered hearing something about sharpening swords with winter's coldest water to make them shine like a mirror, and it reminded her of the chilly Kyoto winters: punishingly cold, but nonetheless lovely.

"Your tea...," said the woman from earlier. It really did take her a long time to bring the tea, just like Oba said it would. She had steamed wheat buns with her as well.

After she left, Iwako said, "These are from Fuuka, aren't they? The little shop on Sawaragicho Street."

"Yeah, they're the sweet buns they wrap in those bamboo leaves. Do you like them?" Oba asked.

"I love them."

After removing the bamboo leaf, she slid the smooth bun into her mouth; it was moist and subtly sweet. As she relished the elegant taste, she rolled up the bamboo leaf and said, "This smells so wonderful, too..."

"It's bamboo from deep in Kurama. Apparently, you can't get leaves that look as pretty and smell as good as these anywhere else."

There didn't seem to be anyone in the house; it was silent except for the occasional passing car heading toward Matsuo.

"This restaurant didn't even have a sign outside."

"Yeah, they don't accept unfamiliar customers. You need a regular to introduce you before you can eat here. And there's just two tables. They apparently use only what they've got inside the house. You can even spend the night, too. They fill the bath in the afternoon. It's an ancient bath, probably haunted."

"What kind of people come here?"

"Folks like us, plus the occasional celebrity, apparently. Kyoto's a big town, though. There are tons of places like this."

"You sure know a lot."

"About Kyoto?"

"About the women you bring here."

"You're the only one, Iwako. I've told you that countless times."

"And I wanted to hear you say it again, so I'll keep on bringing it up."

"You're so cute," Oba teased before checking his watch. "You must be hungry, right?"

"I am, but I'm all right waiting if the food's going to be that good."

"I know I need to relax while we're here, but it's just a habit of mine. Can't help but constantly check my watch when things are this slow."

Oba was a relatively laid-back, calm man, but even he would get antsy every so often. The service here really was moving in slow motion.

"Are you okay for time?" Iwako asked, worried.

"Yeah, I'm fine today. No hurry at all. I'm sure you were really busy today, though."

Iwako had been working half days on Saturdays lately, so if they were going to meet in Kyoto, it had to be on a Saturday. Oba didn't go out at night or on Sundays.

"I already had plans with someone earlier, so this worked out perfectly," said Iwako.

Last night, Iwako's older sister called her about a potential husband she wanted to set Iwako up with. She told her sister she had no intention of getting married.

"Come on, let's not get ahead of ourselves," her sister chided. *"At least listen to what I have to say before you shut me down. Be grateful when people try to show you a little kindness."* Then she asked, *"Can I at least show you a picture of him?"*

"Sorry, but I don't think that's going to change my mind."

"I'll get us a seat at a café near your work tomorrow, so meet me after you're done for the day."

Her sister didn't even wait for a reply, so Iwako had no choice but to meet up with her. She tried to decline without upsetting her sister.

"He's a regular at my hubby's factory. Lost his wife last year. He lives with his mother and two daughters now, but both daughters are about to get married, so I figured you might as well marry the guy. It sure beats getting old alone. Plus, he's rich."

"I don't need money, and I'm not worried about growing old alone, either. Besides, I plan on putting myself in a home whenever I get too old to move anyway."

"You can't be serious."

"I'm very self-centered. There's no way I'd to be able to move in with someone and make compromises. Sorry, Sis."

"So, it's a no, huh? Shame. I really thought he'd make a good match for you. He's fifty-three. His blood pressure's a little high, but he's in good health for the most part."

"I can't even cook or anything like that. I just wouldn't make a good wife," Iwako had claimed, putting an end to the conversation.

Iwako actually liked to cook, and she wasn't against doing chores around the house from time to time, but she wasn't interested in doing any of that for anyone else. She never even entertained the idea of bringing Oba back to her apartment. In fact, the thought of cooking dinner for him and making him miso soup in the morning never crossed her mind. She wasn't going to pretend to be someone's wife or engage in any marital traditions.

Iwako's sister tried to emphasize how she should worry about her future, but Iwako had received some inheritance money when their father passed away. She'd been investing that money wisely, so her savings hadn't diminished in the slightest. One of the men in accounting at her job loved talking about stocks and making money, and he always shared what he knew with her, so Iwako learned how to invest properly. She took out a loan for an apartment in Osaka's Higashi Ward, which she was renting out. She was out almost all day, so she wasn't planning on ever living there herself. It was an investment to her. She never mentioned it to her siblings, though. They used to say, "You've saved up a small fortune. I can smell it," but when they saw how frugally she lived, they figured she must be barely getting by on her father's inheritance. Even her brother, who was working at a store that sold construction materials, stopped asking her to lend him money.

Truth be told, Iwako had made a killing during the huge surge in stock prices earlier that year and had doubled her financial standing. But she didn't tell anyone that, of course. She wasn't planning on opening a shop or doing any sort of business on her own, either. She was fine with keeping her fortune a secret and being "that clerk" for as long as Yamatake Fabrics stayed in business. Not even Oba knew about this talent of hers, although her confidence probably helped create a part of her charm.

Just like how Iwako didn't tell Oba about her finances, she also didn't tell him that she was constantly working on her body in every way she could. She didn't have any real dental problems but nonetheless went to the dentist often to get her teeth cleaned and whitened. She took meticulous care of herself by frequenting saunas and massage parlors. There was nothing she could do to prevent aging, but she could dress nicely and appropriately to make it less obvious. She also had five drinks a night because she heard that sake moisturized the skin and made it glow.

However, there was something that made her skin glow more than any sake, and that something was men. A lifelong bachelorette, Iwako no longer dreamed of getting married. And with that dream gone, she felt positively liberated. Not that she would admit as much in public.

The food had finally arrived: spikenard and broiled butterfish preserved in miso, along with assorted sweet shrimp, icefish, and rock tripe as well. Then came the final dish.

"Careful, it's hot...," the woman warned as she placed the sea bream with turnips on the table. They were served in beautiful, heavy bowls covered in rising steam.

"This will definitely warm us up," Oba commented in delight. "Here."

He handed Iwako a cup. It was Kiyomizu ware, very thin and almost see-through. Then he poured her a light-gold-colored liquor, and she poured him a cup as well.

I wonder how many more times we'll do something like this, Iwako thought as she took a sip. *I could die right now and not regret a thing.*

Before Kuno, Iwako had dated younger men but didn't feel a connection with any of them, just like she hadn't with Kuno, either. They were so young and shameless, and although Iwako liked their intensity, young men simply did nothing for her. After they did the deed, all that followed was silence as they put their clothes back on. It made her begin to wonder: *What goes on in that empty head of his?*

But nothing felt lacking with Oba. Iwako took a bite of her sweet shrimp, which was so cold she could feel her teeth tingle. As the flavor tickled her tongue, she shared a mirthful smile with Oba.

"…Ooh, this is delicious," she said.

"Yeah, it really is. Reminds me of you."

"How exactly?"

"Reminds me of how you taste…down there."

"You're such a pervert."

She loved their dirty exchanges, too.

"The sake is so smooth. It was locally brewed in Fushimi."

"There's still food coming, right?"

"Yeah, but it's going to be a while. It'll come in slow waves. But we can enjoy ourselves until nighttime. Apparently, we have the room across the hall, too."

Iwako got the feeling she was already red in the face from the alcohol and pretended she didn't hear Oba.

"It's really quiet here," she commented while opening another window. The trees were in full leaf and blocking the view of the street, but it was so cold that no one was likely out sightseeing today. The freezing, cloudy sky made it look like evening had already come.

Oba looked at the hanging scroll in the alcove.

"Looks like some priest's calligraphy," he commented. "A lot of their calligraphy is so abstract."

"I think it says 'white clouds'?"

"There's something on the bottom about Arashiyama."

Oba said he'd practiced calligraphy once upon a time, but he hated it. He claimed it made him feel exhausted.

"I used to do a little calligraphy myself, but I felt the same way. I couldn't relax at all. Maybe it had something to do with my inability to concentrate, but I felt like I was wasting my time trying to copy exactly how the instructor wrote. Calligraphy was actually frustrating because I'd remember all the things that annoyed me," Iwako said, causing Oba to erupt with laughter.

"Yeah, it really does that to you for whatever reason. The only time I feel like I can do calligraphy is when I'm feeling energetic and aggressive. Know what I mean? And I definitely can't do it if I'm thinking about you, Iwako. That'd put me in a trance. My handwriting's still garbage, and I can't even hold a pen properly. Doing calligraphy helped me realize how angry I can get."

"Drawing's different, though. I used to take a watercolor painting class and muddied up the paper however I wanted. Drawing and painting are mindless fun."

"Maybe you're right. I checked out a haiku meetup once, but it was brutal. Getting any good at poetry seemed like more effort than it was worth, and all the novices who sucked at it put more effort into gossiping than getting better."

Oba also enjoyed photography and had quit playing golf. Apparently, he'd gotten so busy that all of his hobbies were on hold for the moment.

"You're the only thing on my mind, Iwako," he said insouciantly.

She smiled without offering a reply, instead listening carefully to those words and keeping them close to her heart. Iwako treated each meeting with Oba as if it were their last, so seeing him again always felt like a dream come true.

She secretly imagined her and Oba like a couple the night before a suicide pact and thus made sure to indulge in every pleasurable moment she spent with him. Simply meeting a man who made her feel this way made Iwako the happiest woman in the world. Their idle conversations were the icing on top.

Even after taking their time and finishing their plates, the next course still hadn't arrived. Oba remained calm, though.

"Rushing them won't solve anything. They can only do so much with the few people who work here."

Iwako stood in front of the sink. The door to the room Oba had mentioned was shut, but no one appeared to be inside, so she cautiously slid it open. The room had an old-fashioned screen propped up like a partition and a futon rolled out on the floor. This was the first time she'd ever heard of a home welcoming guests so inconspicuously. After all, she usually met Oba at a hotel in the city.

The bathroom—or rather, the small lavatory where the sink was—was extremely cold. Parts of Arashiyama visible from the window sparkled white with snow. After finishing her business, Iwako randomly remembered that she had to call the real estate agent in Mino tomorrow because she'd heard that a somewhat valuable piece of property was about to go on the market. If everything checked out, she planned on purchasing it and building a house there to rent out. That said, making money would never be her dream, nor did she have any intentions of lavishing funds on a man. Money was important. And after seeing her sister working at an iron foundry, her skin rough and covered in metal powder, Iwako became convinced that money was her sole recourse.

Iwako wasn't interested in buying a man's affections, either. She'd already had her share of men who made the woman pay for their dates, just like the last younger man she went out with.

When it came to her finances, she didn't even let her guard down around Oba. She never told him about her fortune. Iwako felt she might lend him some cash if he asked, but that was strictly a *what if.* Deep down, she knew she would never do such a thing. It wasn't her style. She could imagine herself selling her body for cash before ever financially supporting a man. Her love for Oba was completely separate.

"Look, it's snowing. No wonder it's so cold."

By the time they finished their meal and took a bath, it was already past five PM.

Oba was in his yukata when he opened the window and made that charming remark. The room with the partition was even quainter than it had seemed, and the carvings above the sliding partitions were completely black from oxidation. There was no view of the mountains; the only things visible outside were the dense trees up against the window, the snow gently falling between the branches. Evening was early this time of year.

Oba looked stunning in his yukata. He was probably used to wearing one around the house. His abs and glutes stuck out through the fabric, and tightening his sash made his yukata fit snug like a glove. Iwako was already under the covers in the futon, gazing at Oba's backside.

Whenever they went to the hotel right by Lake Biwa or the Royal Hotel in Osaka, she took her time enjoying their encounter as if that were their last. Each time they did meet, it would feel like a distant memory from a past life. There was no "till death do us part." Iwako didn't believe that lovers were reunited in an afterlife. She felt that any bonds people had became undone when they died.

Perhaps Oba was right when he said, "There's never any 'to be continued' with you. It always comes to an end, then the next time I see you, it's a fresh start."

Iwako shot him a sultry gaze. Her eyes were wicked, even fiendish. She loved the careful way he touched her along with his wild curiosity.

Oba slipped into the warm futon on the floor with her. As his manly hand pulled off her sash, Iwako's heart started racing like usual, as if this were her first time all over again. She suddenly grabbed his wrist, not even knowing what she was doing herself, and tried to stop him.

"Once this right here starts fading to gray...," Oba whispered gently above Iwako as his finger softly traced the edges of the hollow between her legs, "...that's when the real fun starts between a man and a woman. This is where it begins. Let's enjoy this for as long as we can, until the bitter end..."

Iwako didn't know what tomorrow was going to bring. She found herself lying on her back, gently stripped of her yukata. Her throat became parched from the shyness this act still brought her. She felt as if she could hear the snow falling.

Commentary

AMY YAMADA

Sometimes, my ex calls me up. I've never really had any bad break-ups before, so our conversations usually fill me with warmth and happiness.

"Is now a good time to talk?"

I like men with manners. I like it when the conversation starts polite until I gradually start sensing some vague notes of naughtiness from the other end of the line. It's exhilarating. I love talking on the phone with men who make me slightly regret we ever broke up in the first place. This one probably has a wife or a cute girlfriend now, and yet he still conscientiously calls this woman he used to date—a woman he once chose and who chose him as well. There's a hint of danger to the relationship, which makes it all the more fun.

Whenever an ex calls me, I rest my head on my current partner's lap while he's napping and thoroughly enjoy the shameless chatting. As I engage in this extended phone conversation with my ex, I feel a sense of security that the lap I'm lying in is going to be by my side for as long as I need him. Perhaps my ex is lying in a cute woman's lap while he's talking to me, too.

All of a sudden, my partner rolls over in his sleep, perhaps uncomfortable from the weight of my head. I lift my head and glance back at him when I'm hit with a feeling like I'm doing something that maybe I shouldn't be. "Sorry," I mutter while imagining myself sticking my tongue out at him. "I won't be long. Just a few more minutes." I simply cannot hang up; the phone conversation continues.

It's similar to how I feel when I read Seiko Tanabe's novels. Like, *Oh no, I shouldn't do this* but also, *Ah, this is so nice.* I never regret those feelings. The stories warm my heart, but they make my heart ache as well, and those emotions give me a sense of relief.

Tanabe's work stimulates something deep within me that I've long forgotten, just like in the story where the protagonist's ex calls her out of the blue. At times, to my surprise, it's as if the story is identifying truths I was never even aware of. I find myself a bit flustered when the stories expose things about me that haven't crossed my mind even once.

This novel is filled with various short stories like that. Kozue in "I Always Had a Feeling" is a dreamer who finds herself attracted to her sister's fiancé a little too much, which causes her to feel embarrassed and act out. She pretends not to notice, and yet she knows all too well how she really feels. She knows that's not something she's supposed to feel, and it makes her even more self-conscious, which in turn makes her want to hide those feelings further. Reading Kozue's story made me clasp my hand over my mouth from the realization that this was a reflection of me.

Seeing Mimi put her own satisfaction second in "Men Hate Muffins" felt like having someone point out something similar inside us that we all share, which is startling, to say the least.

"Until It Snows" is a hopeful story that shows us someone, who appears to be a bland middle-aged woman, living her best life in secret. In "Josee," she uses the phrase *We're a couple of bodies* to describe the frustration of not being able to convey what it feels like to be happy, something I couldn't help but agree with. All women can relate to these short stories, which make us snap our fingers, or let out a surprised little shout, or say to ourselves, "I know how that feels" with a hint of sorrow in our voices. We even relish the feeling.

I'm particularly fond of the short story "Love's Coffin." The protagonist, Une, has a wonderful split personality. Once a woman realizes she has a split personality, she either turns to self-loathing or starts loving herself even more. It all depends on what kind of woman she is. An unaccomplished woman never develops a wonderful split personality, nor is she capable of reflecting on it even if she realizes she has two personalities. Plus, it takes a wonderful man to shape a woman into someone with a wonderful split personality. An idiot would only turn her into a traitor. Of course, the woman can't be an idiot, either. Someone with a wonderful split personality must be talented.

In a way, all of Seiko Tanabe's protagonists are blessed with such talent: a talent to love life.

I often find myself burying my nose in her novels whenever I'm feeling aggravated or downhearted. They teach me how to enjoy my own life. No other books can teach me that, no matter how advanced or philosophical they may be. All they do is confuse my empty head. How many things out there can you say make you happy, without the need of some hard-to-understand theory about happiness? And how many people out there don't even know these things exist? I would never recommend any of Seiko Tanabe's novels to them. It'd be a waste.

My ex who called me earlier asked me, *"What are you doing now?"*

"I'm reading one of Seiko Tanabe's novels."

He immediately started cackling. *"Again? I don't understand how you enjoy those things so much."*

And I don't care that he doesn't understand. I would never want a man to understand the thrill. Meanwhile, I'm becoming a nicer person thanks to Seiko Tanabe's works. My heart is filled with a warm regret—the regret I felt for having forgotten to tell this ex certain things. But I'll set those regrets aside, because I have to give the best leftovers to the man I'm currently with.

I bet my ex thinks I'm still hiding the best-smelling leftovers, which is why our phone calls are always long. He wants to know what that smell is. I usually never call him myself. I always think, *What if a woman picks up instead?* I'm a very timid person, to be honest. Not that my ex realizes, of course. I'm always shameless and slightly charming whenever I talk to him on the phone in front of my current partner. My ex has no idea that I only let on that I'm a timid person as a last resort. And just like that, my personality gradually splits into two. Of course, I still have a long way to go before I become someone as wonderful as the women with split personalities in Seiko Tanabe's stories, but I can't deny that I feel a glimmer of hope that I might someday be like them: a mature woman who can casually tuck away the possibility that she may hurt the man she loves, just like the protagonist in "Love's Coffin."

I wrote that Seiko Tanabe's novels stimulate something long forgotten in the depths of my heart. On that note, there's one particular memory I can still recall even now: It involves a bar of chocolate.

I was three years old and living in Sapporo with my parents. My mother was in the hospital giving birth to my little sister. She was there for an extremely long time, since it was apparently a difficult delivery.

My father and I had it rough while she was gone. We had just moved here and didn't know anyone who could help us cook us dinner, nor did we have any relatives who lived nearby. My mother's younger sister came all the way to this cold region to look after me for the second half of my mother's hospital stay. Until then, my young father fed me baguettes day in and day out. I had them with butter some days and jam others but started to get fed up with it all.

I watched it snow outside and idly thought about how unlucky I was. But when I looked to my noble, courageous father, I had to give up on the idea that I was doomed to misfortune. I started to feel terrifyingly indifferent about it all, at least as much as a three-year-old could. Apparently, that puzzled my aunt.

Eventually, my mother came home. Her face was glowing and radiant, and in her arms was a monkey-like baby. I had no idea what to do. I felt detached: *Oh, so this is what my mother abandoned me for.*

"Futaba"—my real name—"was such an angel while you were gone," my aunt gushed. My father was overjoyed the moment he saw his brand-new child and couldn't take his hands off her.

My mother came over to me as I sat in silence in front of the potbelly stove. "Sorry I was gone for so long," she said, patting me on my head. And then she gave me a chocolate bar and told me it was my reward. It was one of those Japanese chocolate bars I'm sure everyone is familiar with—the ones that look like a Hershey's bar.

I started eating it. "She's such a good girl," I heard my aunt say. The sweetness and bitterness from the chocolate slowly spread throughout my mouth as I slowly came to a realization: They should have treated me like this the whole time. Things would've been easier if they'd rewarded me sooner.

I ate the chocolate as I wordlessly cried to myself. The tears were comforting and warm, and before I realized it, I was sobbing to the point of hiccupping. All the adults in the room looked at me. My father stood stock-still in confusion while my mother cradled me in her arms, and my aunt burst out laughing. That day, I learned one way to make life more enjoyable.